"I'm supposed to be taking care of your leg," she whispered.

He lifted his head, that drawl of hers singing through his head. "The leg's all better. Now it's my turn to take care of you."

Kate's glance went to his towel.

"I don't think you need to worry about your modesty anymore, do you?" Her fingers went to the tucked-in portion and he moved to stop her before it was too late.

"Don't."

The word was a harsh command, and she blinked up at him, surprise written across her face.

He nodded toward the overhead light, forcing his voice to soften. "Can you turn that light off?"

Dear Reader

Changes in life. We all go through them. Some of those changes make us stronger…and some of them have the power to bring us to our knees. The hero and heroine in THE LONE WOLF'S CRAVING, part two of the *Men of Honour* duet, are both going through such a change. They each struggle with the realisation that their lives will be forever altered as a result. They must make a choice: accept what the future holds and move forward, or rail against fate and remain trapped in a vicious cycle of anger and bitterness.

Thank you for joining Luke and Kate as they face the heartbreak that comes with change and search for the courage to overcome. Best of all—they find love along the way. I hope you enjoy reading about their journey as much as I enjoyed writing about it!

Much love

Tina Beckett

Book One of the *Men of Honour* duet

THE WIFE HE NEVER FORGOT by Anne Fraser

is also available this month
from Mills & Boon® Medical Romance™

THE
LONE WOLF'S
CRAVING

BY
TINA BECKETT

MILLS
BOON

First published in Great Britain 2013
by Mills & Boon, an imprint of Harlequin (UK) Limited.
Harlequin (UK) Limited, Eton House, 18-24 Paradise Road,
Richmond, Surrey TW9 1SR

© Tina Beckett 2013

ISBN: 978 0 263 23376 6

Harlequin (UK) policy is to use papers that are natural, renewable and recyclable products and made from wood grown in sustainable forests. The logging and manufacturing process conform to the legal environmental regulations of the country of origin.

Printed and bound in Great Britain
by CPI Antony Rowe, Chippenham, Wiltshire

Born to a family that was always on the move, **Tina Beckett** learned to pack a suitcase almost before she knew how to tie her shoes. Fortunately she met a man who also loved to travel, and she snapped him right up. Married for over twenty years, Tina has three wonderful children and has lived in gorgeous places such as Portugal and Brazil.

Living where English reading material is difficult to find has its drawbacks, however. Tina had to come up with creative ways to satisfy her love for romance novels, so she picked up her pen and tried writing one. After her tenth book she realised she was hooked. She was officially a writer.

A three-times Golden Heart finalist, and fluent in Portuguese, Tina now divides her time between the United States and Brazil. She loves to use exotic locales as the backdrop for many of her stories. When she's not writing you can find her either on horseback or soldering stained glass panels for her home.

Tina loves to hear from readers. You can contact her through her website or 'friend' her on Facebook.

Recent titles by the same author:

NYC ANGELS: FLIRTING WITH DANGER*
ONE NIGHT THAT CHANGED EVERYTHING
THE MAN WHO WOULDN'T MARRY
DOCTOR'S MILE-HIGH FLING
DOCTOR'S GUIDE TO DATING IN THE JUNGLE

NYC Angels

To those who have faced life-altering events.
May you always find the strength to face the future.

CHAPTER ONE

Had she figured out who he was *before* or *after* she'd had sex with him?

Because Dr. Lucas Blackman sure as hell hadn't known the petite blonde American wandering around his emergency room was his wartime hero's long-lost daughter. Not when he'd pressed her against the wall in the supply closet and buried himself inside her. Not after it was over. In fact, she'd disappeared as quickly as she'd come.

He groaned at the unintended pun. And then again as memories of his actions yesterday washed over him: the snick of the lock; the fumbling with clothing; along with every second of pounding urgency that had happened afterward. Damn it if he wouldn't do it all over again, even knowing what he did now. That she'd probably used him to get what she'd wanted.

Not that he'd been the slightest bit hesitant at the time.

And that memory made his already sucky day even suckier. Walking to the physical therapy center to see how his friend was doing, and seeing the woman he'd had the best sex with—well, in a long damn time—standing beside him sent shock waves rolling through him that rooted him to the spot. Nick introducing her to one of the therapists as his daughter just made it that much worse.

He decided to back away while he still could.

Then her eyes met his and flitted away, making a painless getaway impossible. He could swear he saw a trace of guilt in the deep blue depths. At what? Their naughty rendezvous? At having coffee with him for the last two mornings, all the while being coy and secretive about her reasons for visiting the hospital?

Nick spied him, calling him over just as the therapist disappeared back into the rehabilitation center. His friend winced slightly as he rotated his upper body, his surgery site evidently still tender. "Come and meet Kate—er, Katherine." His friend glanced at her in question. "My daughter."

"Kate," she answered in the same low Southern drawl that had drawn him like a moth to a flame. First in the hospital cafeteria. Then in the tiny supply closet. He could still her soft moans as he'd taken her. Who knew a drawl during sex could be so damned hot. She'd reminded him of warm lazy summers by the lake, of county fairs and high school football games.

All things American.

He'd been homesick yesterday and devastated after losing a patient in the E.R., and there she'd been. As if sent just to ease his pain. And she had. She'd sent him right over the edge.

And she was his hero's daughter. The man who'd once saved his life. *His daughter!*

Hell, today had officially taken a nosedive.

He moved closer and held out his hand, forcing her to do the polite thing and take it. When she tried for a quick grip and release, he curled his fingers around hers and held on, his thumb gliding over her soft skin.

Where do you think you're going, Miss Kate? No running away for you. Not this time.

She'd taken off out of that supply closet like a bat out of hell. Before he'd even finished catching his breath. Just like Cinderella. Only she hadn't left a shoe behind. Just a pair of lacy panties, which he'd shoved into the pocket of his slacks before heading out the door. By then she had been long gone.

"Yes, Kate and I have already been..." he let his deliberate pause and raised brows get his message across, before completing the phrase "...thoroughly introduced."

Her soft gasp said his inference had hit its mark.

Nick glanced from one to the other. "You have? When?"

"Yesterday," she said, stretching the truth. Luke released her hand, watching as she took one step back, and then another. "I was looking for your room and he...helped me."

Helped her.

Oh, he'd helped her all right. Right up onto the scrub sink in the corner of the tiny closet. *After* he'd hiked her skirt up around her waist. He swallowed. What had happened after that was a blur.

One he'd never forget for as long as he lived.

A muscle in his jaw clenched as he stared at her and said, "I didn't know who you were at the time."

"I—I know. And I'm sorry. I should have said something."

So she *had* known he was Nick's doctor, and probably that they were friends, as well. A wave of disappointment washed over him. He should be used to it by now. The "being used" part, that was. His mother hadn't thought twice about using him to collect her monthly welfare checks, all the while earning a small fortune on the side by sleeping with other men. His father hadn't hesitated before sending him into a store to pick up a thing or two—without paying for it, of course.

And now Kate.

As cynical as Luke thought he was, he hadn't managed to see past those baby blues to the person beneath her melt-in-your-mouth sweetness.

And, damn, had she ever melted. The second his lips had met hers.

He hardened everything that wasn't already hard. "Yes. You should have."

She hadn't been in the cafeteria this morning, like she had the past couple of mornings, so he'd assumed he'd never see her again. Yet here she was. All twitchy and apologetic. And the only thing he wanted to do was yank her out of the room and find that closet all over again.

Not going to happen.

Nick stretched his back. "Well, I should probably head in to my physical therapy session."

That was his cue to leave. "And I have some patients to see so, if you'll excuse me, I'll head back."

"Wait! I want to…"

When he turned his head to look at her, Kate's teeth were digging into that delectable lower lip, as if trying to keep the rest of her sentence from coming out in a rush.

She glanced at Nick. "I'll come back when you're finished with therapy, if that's okay."

"Of course." The other man touched her arm. "It was good to finally meet you in person."

Well, Luke wasn't the only sucker, it would appear. She'd had his savior fooled, as well.

By the time he realized she meant to follow him down the hallway, it was too late to stop her. So as soon as they were a safe distance away, he turned to face her, propping one shoulder against the long narrow wall in the hallway to take some of the pressure off his now aching leg.

Pale silky hair, with just the slightest hint of a wave, fell over her shoulders, caressing her collarbone with every turn of her head. He remembered licking along that very spot.

He forced his gaze back to her eyes. "Yes?"

"I...I wanted explain." Her words tumbled over themselves. "I don't normally... I don't *ever*..." The flourish of a hand finished her thought.

She didn't normally sneak off and "do" her father's doctors?

"And you think I should know this because...?"

"I don't want you to think badly of me." Her hands caught each other, fingers twisting together.

She was nervous. Embarrassed by what they'd done. He stood upright before the realization could affect him. "I don't really even know you, so why does it matter?"

She flinched. "I guess it doesn't. But you're Ni—my father's doctor. I'd rather you didn't say anything to him about yesterday."

"I'm not."

"You're not going to tell him?"

"I'm not Nick's doctor. Not anymore."

Her breath hissed out. "So you *are* going to tell him...about us?"

And risk being shipped home to the States on the first available flight out of London? Not likely. He'd fought too hard to get this position. "No, I'm not going to tell him."

"Thank you." Her whole body went slack with relief. "I appreciate it. How's he doing, by the way? Was the surgery a success?"

That same feeling of unease washed over him. Surely she didn't think their time together had been a game-changer? "I'm afraid I can't give out that kind of information."

"But I'm his daughter."

"You're not listed as his next of kin."

"Because I've only just met the man."

And Luke had just barely met her. That hadn't stopped her from wrapping her legs around his waist. And it certainly wasn't keeping him from wanting to relive that moment…a whole lot slower this time. Definitely not something he wanted her to know.

"That's not my problem."

"Okay, I get it. You can't give me any details. But his life isn't in danger anymore, right?"

Luke made a *tsk* noise low in his throat, trying to keep his irritation from showing. The feeling of being used grew at her persistence. "Get him to add you to his list of relatives, and then we'll talk."

"You can't be serious."

"Oh, but I am." Despite his annoyance, his fingers itched to brush across that smooth, pale cheek and watch it come to life beneath his touch. Except he knew her skin wasn't the only thing that would come to life. Something else he didn't want her to realize.

"So, if he'll admit to being my father—in writing—you can tell me what's going on?"

He inclined his head. "It's a start. As long as he's okay with it." He held up a hand. "Which also has to be in writing."

Her lips thinned. "And if he refuses?"

"Then I can't tell you a blessed thing. Now, if you'll excuse me…"

She hesitated, her mouth opening as if ready to argue further, then she snapped it shut again, hitching her purse higher on her shoulder. "If that's the way you want it."

"I don't make the rules."

But he sure didn't mind breaking them. Hadn't he already proved that in the supply closet?

"Of course you don't."

He couldn't prevent the twitch of his lips at her waspish tone. She might be all peaches and cream on the surface, but underneath she had all the fire of a good Indian curry. You didn't notice it until the first three or four bites, but your tongue remembered the flavor long after you'd finished your meal.

Just like he'd remember the flavor of Kate's lips.

She blinked then swung away from him, preparing to walk back toward the physical therapy center.

For some reason he couldn't let her slip away without making her squirm one last time. "Oh, Kate, I almost forgot."

She turned back toward him. "Yes?"

He gave her a slow, wolfish smile. "I still have your panties."

He had her panties.

What had she expected her to do about it? Hold out her hand and demand he give them back to her right there at the hospital?

Kate ran her wrists under the cool stream of water in her hotel room, hoping to soothe her burning skin. It did no good.

God. What had she been thinking? Men like Dr. Luke Blackman were so far out of her league.

What did she do now? Call and make an appointment to pick up her errant piece of clothing? Or did he plan to keep them as a trophy?

And just where did he have them? At home? In his desk drawer? Above the deep sink with the words *Kate was nailed here* penned beneath them?

She held her wet hands to her cheeks and stared into the mirror, remembering the feel of his fingers on her skin as he'd yanked those very panties down her thighs…his eyes never leaving hers. Then he'd tossed them aside and reached for her hips…lifted her onto the sink.

A wave of heat rushed over her body. Kate had never in her life experienced anything so frighteningly sensual in her life. It had all been over in a matter of minutes. But she knew instinctively she'd never experience anything like that ever again.

She stared into the eyes reflected back at her.

She didn't look any different on the outside. Not a single scorch mark lingered on her skin, although she could still feel each and every place his lips had lingered.

Little had she known all those months ago that the picture and accompanying letter she'd found in a shoebox in her mother's closet—along with letters from scores of other men—would lead her to discover that the father she'd grown up with wasn't her biological father. Or that all her pent-up anger and frustration over the lies by those closest to her would build to the point that it had sought release—no matter what the source.

Luke had been the only person handy at the time.

She'd exploded all right. In a most delicious way.

And now she had to live with the consequences. At least, the emotional ones. Luke had taken care of the physical ones, muttering about the need for birth control, even though her mind hadn't exactly been up to the subject of unwanted pregnancies.

But thank heavens he'd taken precautions. Luke wouldn't need to disappear from his kid's life without a trace, like Nick had. And Kate wouldn't have to lie to her own child about his or her origins—about who its father was. Her eyes moistened. She wouldn't have to die—like her mother had—in order for her child to know the truth.

And most important of all, the only person in the entire world who'd have to live with the consequences of what she'd done in that supply closet...was herself.

CHAPTER TWO

"SHE HATES ME."

Perched on one of the chairs that lined the glass wall of the therapy center, Nick's bald statement took him by surprise. Luke didn't have to ask who his friend was referring to.

"No, she doesn't. When she was here yesterday, she seemed…worried." That was as good a word as any.

His friend's jaw tightened. "I wish I could believe that. That's not the vibe she was giving off when I met her."

"It's a shock, I'm sure. You said she only learned about your existence a month ago, after she found a picture?"

"That's what she said." Nick scrubbed a hand over his head, making his hair stick up at odd angles. "I had a fling with a tourist just before I shipped out with my unit. She'd taken some pictures of us with her camera over the course of the evening. Large quantities of alcohol were involved, so I'm a bit fuzzy on all the details. Anyway, I left her a note the next day before I headed out. I had no idea the woman had got pregnant that night until much later."

"You've had contact with the woman?"

"Not since that day. Kate says she died six months ago." Something flashed through his eyes. Regret?

"And she's just now decided to find you?"

He gave a hard laugh. "She found the picture and my note stuffed in a shoebox. She got the bloke who raised her to admit he wasn't her real father." One shoulder went up. "She came looking for me at the house while I was in the hospital. Nearly ruined things for me and Tiggy in the process."

"Ouch." Kate did seem to have the ability to stir up trouble wherever she went. He hadn't slept much for the past two nights. "Things are okay between you and your wife now, though?"

Nick nodded, a smile curving his lips. "She's pregnant. I never thought I'd want kids, and now I find I have a grown daughter as well as a baby on the way."

"Congratulations!"

"I guess."

"Come on, Nick. What more could you ask for?"

"I could ask for my daughter to give me a chance."

"I'm sure she'll come round. She asked how you were doing. I couldn't tell her anything because of patient confidentiality." He paused. "Maybe I could talk to her. Tell her you're a regular hero."

Whoa, why the hell had he offered to do that? Being around Kate was not good for his equilibrium, especially now.

"I'm not a hero. Especially not in her eyes."

"She just doesn't know you yet. Maybe you should tell her what you did in the service. For men like me." Luke hated remembering his injury, how he'd had to fight his way back from the depths of despair when he'd realized his leg would never be right again. He knew he should be grateful it was still there. But on the days when it ached like nobody's business, he wished he'd just had it lopped off and been done with it.

"I was doing my job." His friend studied him for a moment. "If she asked you how I was doing, she must care. At least a little."

"Of course she does."

"What did you tell her?"

"That you had to sign off on her being your daughter first, giving the hospital permission before I could share any information."

"That could work…"

He frowned. "I'm not sure I follow."

"If I sign the papers, maybe you could be the one to talk to her for me, like you said. And the medical discussion could turn personal. You could feel her out."

Well, he'd already done that. It wasn't something he should do again if he wanted to maintain his sanity. And definitely not something he wanted to admit to Nick. The man who'd saved his leg could very well rip it back off with his bare hands if he found out what he'd done to his newfound daughter.

"You know," Luke said slowly, "I think it might be better coming from you."

"Didn't you just offer to talk to her for me a few minutes ago?"

Yes, and he'd already decided that was not a good idea. "I'm thinking a father-daughter discussion might be more direct. Just tell her that you shipped out right after you were with her mother and over your years of service you saved a lot of men's lives."

"It would be stronger coming from a friend." Nick cocked his head. "One of those very people I saved."

Wow. He'd never expected Nick to play the you-owe-me card. And, in all honesty, he probably wouldn't have now if *he* hadn't offered to talk to Kate, like a damned fool. His fingers went to his leg, a familiar ache reminding him of what could have been had Nick not been there.

"Not fair."

"I know." His friend's voice was low. "But I'm feeling desperate. She's due to leave for the States in a week or two, and I want to make sure things are okay between us before she goes."

"What do you expect me to do? Drop my pants and show her firsthand what a great job you did on my leg?"

He hadn't even done that in the supply closet. He'd simply unzipped and…

Oh, hell. This was not a good idea.

"No pants-dropping allowed. I may have just found out she's my daughter, but that doesn't mean I want you coming on to her. I've heard about your reputation from a couple of the nurses." His voice sharpened a bit. "You're still a hotshot, just like you were ten years ago."

Nick might be surprised. He wasn't guilty of half the stuff floating around the hospital grapevine. And his physical hotshot days were long gone. He might still have the use of his leg, but he'd never be a marathon runner. Or climb the Alps. Or even carry a woman across the threshold. He'd surprised himself by actually getting Kate up onto that sink—although he could lift things just fine, it was walking and lifting together that did him in.

Luckily, he wouldn't have to fess up to what had happened between him and Kate, because that was obviously not something Nick would be thrilled to hear. And Kate didn't want Nick knowing either, judging by her quiet plea in the hallway. "So you don't want me to charm her."

"I want you to talk to her." Nick's voice softened. "Tell her I'm not a bad-boy-love-'em-and-leave-'em type. Just an honest working man who made a mistake. One he regrets."

"So you want someone who you think is a Lothario to tell your daughter *you're* nothing like that."

Nick grinned. "Exactly."

Just then an attractive redhead dressed in scrubs came into the center and dropped a kiss on his friend's cheek. "I thought I'd check up on you. How are you feeling?"

"Better." He nodded at Luke. "Tiggy, you remember Dr. Blackman...Luke."

"Of course. He's the one who called and told me you were in the hospital." She smiled, her eyes crinkling at the corners. "Hello again. I don't know if I've ever thanked you properly for what you did. I'm very grateful."

"I'm glad Nick still had you listed as his next of kin."

"So am I." She laid her hand on her husband's shoulder. "Nick's told me a little about how you met."

Luke tensed, but forced himself to return her smile. "Nothing bad, I hope."

"No, just that you came across each other while in the service. I didn't even know that we did joint missions with the Americans." She took her husband's hand in hers.

So that's what Nick had told her.

No hint that she knew about Nick yanking him from the jaws of death. Or that he'd refused to saw his leg off on the spot, like one of the other medics had wanted to do.

Luke relaxed. He may have told his friend to come clean with Kate about what he'd done in the field, but

Luke himself told very few people about that day. Some of his buddies from his service days knew, but only because they'd been there when it had happened. Luke preferred it that way. Anyone who saw his scars and was brave enough to ask about them got a very watered-down version of what had actually gone down.

Hell. Nick was right. He owed the man a debt he could never repay.

Backing out of talking to Kate seemed pretty selfish in the face of it all. He made a quick decision. "About that favor you asked for. I can't promise anything, but I'll give it a shot. I'll need you to sign the paperwork, so I have an excuse to approach her."

His friend's eyes closed for a second and he took a deep breath before looking back at him. "Thank you. I owe you."

No. He didn't. And that was exactly the point.

Kate frowned as she took the envelope from the man at the front desk. It couldn't be from her father back in Memphis, he'd have simply emailed her if he couldn't reach her. And she didn't know anyone in London except Nick.

Oh, and one very enigmatic doctor.

And she didn't even know him. Just that he made her pulse explode…along with other things. Things she was trying very hard to forget.

Walking toward the twin elevators, she slid a thumb beneath the seal of the envelope and popped open the tab. A single sheet of paper was inside.

Could you call me when you get in? I'm at
20-5555-6731
Thanks, Dr. Lucas Blackman

A wave of panic went through her before she realized it probably wasn't anything related to Nick's health. If it were, he wouldn't have left a note. Then she gulped as she remembered his parting shot from yesterday. This couldn't be about her panties, could it? She'd prefer he just burn them and be done with it. It was just too humiliating to talk about over the phone. Or in person, for that matter.

But if she didn't call, she'd always wonder.

She wasn't sure what kept her from booking a flight out of London. She'd done what she'd come to do: looked her father in the eye and drawn her own conclusions. She'd expected that to be fairly quick and easy, but nothing had gone the way she'd planned.

Nick wasn't the type of person she'd braced herself to find. He hadn't denied being her father—which surprised her—but then again it was kind of hard to deny the obvious. But there was something in his face that made her want to take a step back and rethink her position. Especially in the face of all those other letters she'd found in the shoebox. Did the man who'd raised her even know about those other men?

She hardened her heart. If those closest to her hadn't thought twice about lying to her, why not the man who'd contributed nothing to her life other than his DNA?

Her mom had been trying to spare her feelings, she was sure. But surely with all her grandparents' money, her mother would have been able to track Nick down and tell him about the pregnancy. Or about the baby, once she'd been born. So why hadn't she?

Her mother wasn't here to answer any of those questions. Maybe she would have told her someday, but had never gotten the chance.

Or maybe she knew something about Nick that was

so terrible she hadn't wanted her daughter to have any contact with him. Maybe Nick had…forced her, or something.

She stepped off the elevator. No, she had found the note Nick had left the next morning. He wouldn't have done that if something bad had happened between him and her mother. And her mother certainly wouldn't have saved a picture of them together had that been the case.

Unlocking her door, she went into her room and dropped her purse on the bed. Her suitcase was still packed, sitting on the mahogany luggage rack. She could just shut the lid and leave with everything she'd come with.

Except answers. And, of course, one pair of panties.

Ugh. She smoothed out the note and traced her finger over the bold strokes of handwriting, smiling at the typical doctorlike scribbles. Luckily she'd had to decipher many notes like these during her physical therapy training, and later, with actual patients, to understand what their doctors wanted.

There was nothing for it but to call and find out what he wanted.

She punched the number that would allow her to reach an outside line and then dialed the rest of the digits listed on the note.

"Blackman here."

His voice sounded sharp, hurried. "Oh, I'm sorry. You left me a—"

"Kate?" His tone immediately changed. Softened. "I didn't expect you to call so soon."

She blinked and glanced at the note again. No time stamp. Was it possible he'd left it only a short time ago? "Oh, I…I just got in."

"Listen, I'm swamped right now. But basically your

father's listed you as next of kin and has given me permission to fill you in, if you've got some free time."

"I can be there in a half hour."

There was a pause. "Can we do it somewhere else? I have something of yours I need to return, and I'd rather it not be at the hospital."

If only he'd been that conscientious a couple of days ago.

And meeting him in her hotel room was out of the question. Not because she didn't trust him but because she didn't trust herself. If she'd have sex with him in a public hospital, what would stop her from peeling his clothes off in a private room?

"How about a restaurant?" *No, not a restaurant, dummy.* "I mean a coffee shop."

"A restaurant sounds great." He said something to someone with him then came back to her. "I've really got to go. I'll pick you up when I get off. Say around six this evening."

"Oh, um…"

"Say yes, Kate." His voice had gone all soft and gravelly, and she shivered. It was almost identical to the tone he'd used in the supply room. *Do you want this, Kate?*

She had. She'd said the word that had unleashed them both. And damn if she wasn't about to say it all over again.

"Yes."

CHAPTER THREE

LUKE TURNED HIS car into the hotel, giving a soft whistle as he did. He'd heard of The Claymont—knew it was exclusive and pricey—but had never had any reason to visit before now.

Towering white columns framed an ornate cobble-stone driveway, the swirling pattern in the black-and-white marble chips echoing the curve of the entryway. An intricate coat of arms placed in the middle reminded him of the X on a celebrity red carpet, giving vehicles a definite stopping point. The place oozed opulence—from the lion's-head fountain on a side wall, which splashed water into a rustic concrete trough, to the red-coated doorman who emerged from the interior of the hotel to greet him.

Kate had money. Lots of it.

Which might explain their encounter the other day. Maybe she was one of those cute socialites who got their kicks out of toying with danger.

And their time in that supply closet had definitely been dangerous. It had pushed the boundaries, even for him.

But he also remembered her hesitancy that first day at the entrance of the hospital. She hadn't acted like a spoiled little rich girl.

Maybe her mom had married into money. Nick said Kate's father knew she wasn't his biological daughter, so her mother hadn't used an unwanted pregnancy to trick anyone into marrying her.

She hadn't lied about it.

Except to Kate, evidently. It had to be rough having your world suddenly turned on its head.

He handed the keys of his little MGB to the valet.

"I won't be long," he said.

"Very good, sir."

The front entrance welcomed him, the double doors swishing open with a quiet hiss. What the hell would he do if she invited him up to her room?

It was a question he'd never thought he'd have to ask himself. But Nick was her father, so there would be no more supply closets…and definitely no hotel rooms in his future. He could keep his hands off her, really he could.

"May I help you, sir?"

The guy at the front desk was just as smooth and re-fined as he'd expected. "I'm here to see Kate Bradley."

"One moment." He tapped some buttons on his computer keyboard, but just as he was picking up the hand-set to dial her room, the elevator doors pinged and Kate herself emerged.

The air left his lungs, just as it had the first time he'd seen her. It wasn't so much the way she was dressed as the way she carried herself—although the dark jeans clung in all the right places and the dark green halter-top left her pale shoulders exposed, revealing a smat-tering of freckles.

"Sorry, I wasn't sure where we were going," she said when she reached him.

That soft drawl slid over his body like warm silk. Again.

He noticed the guy behind the desk just stood there, the phone still gripped in his hand. So Luke wasn't the only one who thought the whole damn package was irresistible. When he turned his eyes toward the other man and lifted his brows, the guy put the phone down with a quick click, his face turning red. "Can I get you anything, Ms. Bradley?"

How about a fire extinguisher, so she can put you out?

As if he himself was any better at containing that particular fire.

One side of his mouth quirked. Was Nick absolutely sure this was his kid? Because he just wasn't seeing the resemblance.

Kate smiled at the desk clerk, hiking the shiny metal links of her purse onto her shoulder. "I think I'm good. Thank you, though."

No thinking needed. She *was* good.

Giving himself an internal eye roll, he motioned toward the door. "Are you ready? I know a place a couple of miles from here."

Once in his little car and heading down the road, he noticed Kate flinching periodically as they passed other cars.

"It still seems so strange to be driving on the left. I keep thinking someone is going to honk at us. Or worse."

"You get used to it." Not that she was going to be here long enough for that. So exactly how was he supposed to shine up Nick's halo while avoiding tarnishing his own any further? By returning that little article of clothing she'd left behind a few days ago? "There's a paper bag in the glove box. You might want to take it with you."

She tugged on her seat belt as if needing a bit more breathing space and stared at the latch in front of her. "I think I'll wait until we get back to the hotel, if that's okay. My purse is pretty small."

She knew exactly what was in there. He'd had half a mind to take the easy way out and toss the panties into the garbage, but he hadn't. Luke had never been one to shy away from things that were uncomfortable, even when it had come to his folks' poverty…his dad's drunken anger. He'd just stood there and faced it down unblinking. "Don't forget them. I'd hate the wrong person to go digging through that glove box."

"Like your next conquest?"

Maybe she'd gotten wind of his reputation, as well. He really was going to have to appear a whole lot more boring at work. "I was thinking more along the lines of Nick—your father."

Kate's face drained of all color and she turned to stare at him. "You promised you wouldn't say anything about that."

Hell, the woman really didn't think much of him, did she? Luke rarely gave his word, but when he did, he moved hell and high water to keep it. He'd learned the hard way that most promises were quick on the tongue and easily broken. Not by him, though.

And yet he'd made two pretty big promises in the last couple of days. One to Nick and one to his daughter. "I already told you I'm not going to tell him."

He stopped for a red light, shifting down to first gear and glancing over at her. "What happened at the hospital stays between the two of us—no one's going to hear it from me."

Her eyes closed for a second, and she nodded. "Thank you. I couldn't bear it if anyone thought I was…"

"If anyone thought what?"

"It's not important."

If that soft sigh was anything to go by, it was important. At least, to her. But if she wanted to tell him, she would have. It was probably best to stick to neutral topics anyway, since the purpose of this outing was to discuss Nick's treatment, extol his virtues and then each go their merry way.

The light turned green, and Luke eased back into traffic. "Nick's going to make a full recovery, by the way. He had some shrapnel—leftover from an old wound—that shifted. It got a little too close to his spinal cord for comfort. He's just finishing up his course of physical therapy and then he'll be free to go about his business."

Kate twisted in her seat and stared at him. "That's wonderful. So he won't have any permanent damage?"

"No." Unlike himself, who carried a permanent reminder of his time in Afghanistan. "His physical therapy is taking a little longer than expected because of some nerve damage, but after that he should be good to go."

"Maybe I can help. I'm a physical therapist."

She was? Luke frowned. He'd been thinking along the lines of socialite, so the fact that she was a PT came as a complete surprise. "I don't know…"

"I'm licensed, specializing in LSVT."

Luke's head was still spinning at the revelation as he turned another corner. He'd known plenty of physical therapists, but Kate looked nothing like the professionals who'd hauled his ass out of bed after the injury that had nearly claimed his leg. Who'd propped him up-right and goaded him into taking his first shaky steps.

Although remembering the lean muscles beneath his hands as he'd lifted Kate onto that sink, he shouldn't be *that* surprised. And imagining those hands work-ing on his body…

Good God.

He swallowed. Nick would not be happy to know the thoughts racing through his mind right now. For the life of him, he couldn't think of anything to say, so he asked the obvious question. "LSVT?"

"It's a specialized voice therapy for Parkinson's pa-tients."

Ah, so she wasn't the brute-strength type of ther-apist after all. "Nick will need occupational therapy, not speech."

"Part of LSVT deals with the physical aspects of Parkinson's." Her chin tilted stubbornly.

He tried again. "Your father doesn't *have* Parkin-son's."

"Yes, he does, he's in the early…" She let out a soft sigh. "Oh. That's right. It's still hard for me to think of Nick as my father. I'm sure I could help him, though. I've already checked online, there are several hospitals here in England using LSVT. It could be useful, even though he doesn't have Parkinson's."

What had made her check on that? Was she thinking about staying in London? "I'm sure he's getting every-thing he needs at the hospital's PT center."

"But what about when he's not there? I could help him with some extra exercises…help his wife out with him. Maybe it would give me a chance to get to know him better."

Luke wasn't sure Tiggy would welcome the reminder

that Nick had fathered another child. Especially not in her condition. But it wasn't up to him. That was a decision the couple would have to make on their own.

He pulled into the parking lot of the Indian Palace Restaurant and set the handbrake. "Nick and Tiggy are under a lot of stress right now—with the surgery and everything. Now might not be a good time." Unhooking his seat belt, he waited for her to follow suit. "Listen, we'll eat, and I'll fill you in on his surgery and prognosis, and then you'll have a better grasp of his situation, okay?"

"Good. That'll give me more time to convince you."

Not good. He might not be the one she needed to convince, but all he could think was that it might be fun to let her try, anyway.

Kate took a quick gulp of water and then another, her mouth on fire. The smoldering sensation of swallowing hot coals continued as she sucked air in and out through pursed lips in a desperate effort to get some relief. "Oh, my God..." *Huff, huff.* "That's so good."

The man across from her gave her a quick grin. "Your face is pink. And your accent is really coming through."

"Because I'm on *f-i-ire.*"

She put every Southern bone she had into that last word. The food was just-this-side-of-pain spicy. And she loved it. It was hard to get good Indian food in the States, but Luke had assured her that Londoners loved it. And they were evidently not afraid of a little spice. Or a lot, in this case.

"Well, when you decide to go hot, you go all the way, don't you?"

Kate looked at him sharply, wondering if the amusement in his voice was in regard to the food or if he was talking about something else. She tossed her hair over her shoulder and reached for her napkin, using it to dab the still-burning corners of her mouth. The words had stung, but only because she'd let them.

Her mom had been a wonderful, loving mother, but she'd also been impulsive, throwing her whole being into whatever caught her interest. That had tended to change weekly—even daily. When she'd found Nick's note in that shoebox, it hadn't been the only "call me later" letter. There'd been others. Many of them. If not for the fact that her baby picture had been stapled onto a corner of one of the envelopes, which contained a picture of her mother with a much younger Nick, along with his note, she might never have wondered if the man she'd known as her father was actually her biological father.

Her mom's impulsiveness hadn't been restricted to hobbies and charities, it would seem. It had spilled into other areas. And she'd left a trail of broken hearts along the way. Her dad never seemed to indicate she'd strayed during their marriage. Or maybe he didn't know. Kate had never doubted his deep love for her mother, though. He'd been devoted to her. Her death had devastated them both. She was thankful *she'd* found that box and not her dad. She'd hidden everything except Nick's letter and her photo, which had been when her father had broken down and admitted he'd adopted her after he'd married her mother. She'd been two years old at the time.

All those men. Several of them had clearly not understood why her mother hadn't returned their calls. And she'd kept those letters. Why? As reminders?

God. The last thing she wanted to do was hurt anyone like that.

She glanced at Luke. He seemed well able to take care of himself. Their little fling in the storage closet probably hadn't left the slightest scratch.

Unlike she herself, who was still reeling from her actions. They'd been totally out of character for her.

Or were they? She didn't know anymore.

Dropping her napkin back in her lap, she feigned a sweet smile. "I always say if you're going to do something, you might as well make it worth your while."

He nodded at her plate. "Even if it stings."

"Maybe that's the goal."

His smile faded. "To do something that hurts you?"

"Better than hurting others, don't you think?"

He leaned back in his chair and regarded her for a few seconds, his expression grim. "Absolutely."

What was he thinking about? It didn't matter. The sooner she got this question-and-answer session over with, the better. The man had the ability to get under her skin, and she didn't like it. She'd never had casual sex before, and the last thing she wanted to do was look her mistake in the face repeatedly—no matter how handsome that face might be.

"So, you said Nick put me down on his list of relatives. What made him decide to do that?"

"That's something you'll have to ask him. But I assume it's because you're his daughter, and he's happy to have finally met you."

Something pricked at the back of her mind, raising her suspicions. "At the hospital, you said you weren't Nick's doctor anymore, so why are you the one filling me in on his condition? Why not his current doctor?"

"Because he asked me to."

"Why would he do that?" Her brain worked through the possibilities and came up with the most obvious choice. "You know him, don't you? Outside the hospital, I mean." It seemed like Nick knew everyone, except her.

"Yes."

She picked up her fork but didn't use it. She just stared at the gold-rimmed plate for a moment or two. "Did he know about me at all? Or did my mom never contact him again after their…time together?"

Did she want to know the answer to that? Not really, but she couldn't crawl back inside her shell and act like the past six months hadn't happened. Just like the tree of the knowledge of good and evil, what was known couldn't be *un*known ever again.

A warm hand reached over and covered hers. "I don't know," he said. "But I do know that Nick's a good man."

Really? She'd thought her mother had been a saint, too, until a couple of months ago.

"So you know everything about him, do you?" Nick hadn't seemed all that thrilled to find out he'd fathered a child after a one-night stand. And he'd never mentioned whether or not he'd been married to someone else at the time he'd slept with her mother. Please let it be no. She didn't want that hanging over her mother's memory, as well.

Everything inside her was so jumbled right now. She didn't know what to do or think. Her world had ceased making sense the moment she'd peeked inside that shoebox.

What was the big deal, anyway?

Nick had just had a one-night stand. Okay, well, she'd had a one-*day* stand. So who was she to judge anyone?

Luke's eyes hardened, and he let go of her hand. "No,

I don't know everything about him, but I can tell you he once saved a self-destructive dumbass from himself."

She tried to work through what he meant. Who…

Before she could finish her thought he dragged a hand through his hair and blew out a rough breath. "This dumbass owes him one. Big time."

Oh…*oh!*

She caught his hand, the same way he'd caught hers a few minutes earlier. "You're talking about yourself."

He wrapped his fingers around hers, holding her in place and sending crazy tingles skittering up her arm. And that slow, sexy smile was back full force. "Which word gave me away, Kate? *Self-destructive?* Or *dumbass?*"

"Neither." She was about to lay herself bare before him, and she had no idea why. "It was the talk about owing him. You're not the only one who does. I owe him, too. For my very life."

CHAPTER FOUR

WHY THE HELL had he said anything?

Driving back to the hotel after their meal, he cursed himself for revealing so much. She'd already been warming up to the sparkly image of Nick he'd tried to paint, without needing any additional props. So why had he admitted to owing him?

The second he'd seen the confusion in her eyes, heard the raw vulnerability in her voice, he'd been lost. He'd kept up his crusty, uncaring shell through the rest of the meal, but his insides had turned into a gloppy, gooey mess. Like a marshmallow held a little too close to the fire.

Kate didn't owe Nick. Not the way he did. Yeah, his friend may have donated a few thousand sperm to the making of her, but that had been a rash, spur-of-the-moment act. What the man had done for *him* had been far different. Luke had been awake long enough after his injury to hear brief snatches of a heated argument between Nick—who'd been an army medic at the time—and someone else, their accents placing them as English.

"He'll die, if we don't clamp those vessels right now..."

"...give me a few more minutes here."

"...lose the leg, but save his life..."

"...get your bloody hands off my patient, and give me some room!"

"...Americans would rather have him back alive than in a body bag."

The second Luke's eyes had opened again, and he'd spied the familiar walls of a field hospital, his hands had gone straight to his leg. The sense of relief that had swept through him when his fingers had met thick wads of bandages—instead of empty air—had been enormous. Until he'd seen the actual damage and heard the grim prognosis.

He hadn't been out of the woods, and his leg, even if it could be saved in the long run, would never be the same.

Well, the appendage was still with him, but he wondered sometimes if the trade-off had been worth it.

Even as he thought it, his hand came off the stick shift of his car to massage the twisted muscles, but he stopped short. Kate didn't know exactly how Nick had saved his life. For all she knew, he'd simply kept him from doing anything stupid. No reason for her to know the literal truth.

She hadn't said much as she'd finished her meal and he'd paid the bill. They'd simply talked about Nick's original injury, about why it had flared up after all these years, and what had needed to happen during surgery to give him a shot at a normal life.

He turned a corner, heading toward her hotel. This was it. It was probably the last time he'd ever see her, if he was smart. He'd done what Nick had asked, there was no reason to prolong the inevitable. He glanced over at her and frowned. Her head was against the headrest, eyes closed.

Was she sleeping? He looked at the road, and then back at her. Her throat worked a couple times.

No, she wasn't asleep.

Oh, hell. Surely she wasn't fighting back tears. The sooner he got her back to...

A car from one of the lanes of oncoming traffic suddenly shifted for no apparent reason, its trajectory forming a weird serpentine shape as it drifted farther into their lane. It was coming right toward them!

"Hold on." Luke jerked the steering wheel hard to the left to avoid hitting it head on, the tires of his little car striking the curb hard and bumping up onto it. He braked, glancing into the rearview mirror just as the other vehicle passed them, creeping into the wrong lane yet again. If the idiot didn't gain control, he was going to...

The squeal of tires and the awful crunching sound that followed said the worst had indeed happened.

Luke swore and pushed a button to turn on his hazard lights. "Are you okay?"

"Fine, but... Oh, no!" Kate's eyes were now wide open, her head craning to look behind them.

Grabbing his cell phone from the clip on his belt, he dropped it in her lap. "Dial 999. Tell them we need an ambulance and that there's a doctor at the scene."

Not waiting for her reply, he leaped from the car and half skipped, half sprinted toward the accident scene, trying to override his pain threshold with gritted teeth. Damn it!

He tried to mentally separate the rubberneckers from those involved in the crash. Hell. Not good.

Three cars. No, four.

And there was smoke pouring from one of the vehicles, preventing him from getting a good look at its occupants. He headed toward that one first, seeing someone stagger from the driver's side and collapse onto the road a few feet away. If the smoke was obstructing the view of cars still coming toward them, the already bad accident could turn catastrophic.

He yelled to one of the bystanders, "Can you try signaling a warning to cars that are headed this way?"

He reached the victim who'd fallen, a young male, and crouched down, his leg screaming as the muscles contracted too quickly. He ignored the pain, noting the trickle of blood from the man's mouth was due to a busted lip and not from internal injuries.

Sour fumes hit his nostrils, drifting up his sinus passages.

Alcohol. Shit! This was the idiot who'd swerved into their lane. He wasn't hurt, just drunk.

"How can I help?" A man's voice came from over his shoulder. He glanced back beyond the man who had spoken and saw Kate running toward him, as well. He motioned her back, not needing a million bodies wandering around on a smoky roadway.

"Think you can drag him to the curb, in case his car goes up?" He hated that he had to ask for help, that he couldn't do it himself, but there were people in other cars who might be worse off.

But the man got beneath the drunk's arms and dutifully hauled him away from the smoking vehicle. Luke called out, "Don't let him go anywhere. The police will want to have a word or two with him."

Kate got to him just as he reached the second car. "I called it in. Help is on the way."

He glanced at her, before taking in the occupants of the next car, whose small red hood was now a crumpled mess. "I thought I told you to stay back."

"I know, but I'm strong. I can help."

The inference was plain. She'd seen him hobble down the road. Seen him pass off the first victim to someone else. No time to worry about that now.

He nodded at the backseat of the vehicle, the sudden sound of sirens bearing down on them a welcome relief.

"There's a car seat. Check it for me, will you? But if there's a child, don't move it."

Not waiting for an answer, he went around the front and yanked the driver's-side door open. The unconscious woman inside gasped, her mouth wide open as she sucked down air, the harsh unevenness of the sound sending an ominous chill through him. The edge of the steering wheel—despite the presence of an airbag—pressed against the right side of the woman's chest, which meant the force generated by the impact had traveled through the steering column and into her body.

He gulped, his heart rate spiking off the charts when he noted that with each inspiration the left side of the patient's chest rose in a normal fashion, but a significant portion of her right side collapsed inward instead of expanding—a clear sign that multiple ribs had broken free, preventing her diaphragm from doing its job.

Flail chest. Game-changer.

He needed to get her out of that car. Now.

A uniform appeared at his right, the man ducking his head to take a look. "You the doctor?"

"Yes. I have a critical patient here. Do we have an ETA on the ambulance?"

"One's about a minute out, another's on the way."

"She's first." He nodded at his patient, two fingers automatically going to her carotid artery to take her pulse, his gaze straying to the hand of his watch as he calculated the beats per minute.

"I'll see what I can do." The cop moved away.

"Tell them I need a backboard," he yelled after he'd gotten the count.

Rapid and thready, as he'd expected.

"Kate?" he called, remembering he'd asked her to check out the car seat. "What have you got back there? Anything?"

"Yes, there's a baby. I—I don't know how old she is. She's wrapped in a blanket, and she's breathing. I can't see blood anywhere, but she's unconscious."

"Okay, just stay with her for a few minutes and tell me if there are any changes."

He heard the telltale slam of a truck door nearby. *Thank God*. His mind followed the sound indicators.

Swish. Click. Wheels of a gurney being lowered and snapped into place.

Rattle, rattle, rattle. The stretcher being wheeled across the roadway toward him.

Another head appeared. "What have you got?"

"Probable rib fractures resulting in a flail chest. Pulse one-twenty and thready." He paused for a second before forcing the words out. "I'll need some help getting her out of here, though."

The paramedic blinked, his glance skipping over Luke's face for a second before nodding. "Right."

Luke limped back a pace or two to let the EMTs by, his hand going to his thigh and digging his fingers into the flesh to take his mind off the growing pain. It was nothing in comparison to the life-and-death battle going on inside that car. And she had a child. "There's a baby in the back," he said to the paramedics.

"My partner just had a look. Her vitals are strong. We'll tend to the baby next and bring her with us in the ambulance. Injuries in the other cars appear to be minimal."

"Good." At least he'd made the right call in staying with this particular patient. "Careful with her back and with the ribs on her right side. The steering wheel is still making contact there."

As soon as they'd secured the patient, he turned to Kate. "Do you have your international driver's permit?"

"Yes, why?"

"I need to ride with her in the ambulance, if possible. We're about a block away from the hotel. Just turn right at the next corner. And for heaven's sake, keep to the left. Think you can get there without killing yourself or anyone else?"

"Yes, but what about your car?"

"I'll pick it up later. I don't want to leave it here, and I need to go. Now."

Her glance went to his leg, where his fingers were still working to relieve the cramping. "Are you going to be all right?"

So she *had* noticed. Perfect.

He made his hand go slack, digging into his pocket for his car keys, instead. "I'll be fine."

One of the EMTs called over, "Ready to transport."

Kate reached over and plucked the keys from him. "Go. I'll take care of your car. Call me when you're done, okay?"

CHAPTER FIVE

WHAT WAS WRONG with Luke's leg?

She'd been shocked by the way he'd hurried over to the scene of the accident. He'd had a kind of uneven, hobbling run that had done the job but certainly hadn't looked very comfortable. She'd never noticed him limp before. Had he twisted his ankle in his hurry to get over there?

Hmm...no, his hand had massaged his upper thigh, like he'd been working out a kink. A cramp? Maybe.

But the way he'd lowered his arm the second he'd seen her looking at it didn't fit that scenario, either. Kate put the keys to his car on the table in her hotel room and paced, the thick beige carpet beneath her feet deadening the sound. Glancing at her watch, she saw that it was just after eight. Already dark outside. Who knew how long he'd be at the hospital? He'd seemed to indicate he'd call, although he hadn't actually said the words.

Well, she did have his car. So he'd have to get in touch with her eventually.

Even as she thought it, the phone rang. Wow, that was fast.

She picked up the receiver. "I was wondering how long you'd be."

"Sorry?" The soft, clipped tones bore no resemblance to the low, intense murmur that had sent shivers over her in the supply closet. "Is this Kate, then?"

"Um…yes."

There was a pause. "You sound like her, you know."

Kate realized in a flash who it was and sat on the edge of the bed. "Nick?"

There was another pause, longer this time. "Yes."

She thought there might be a slight edge of hurt to his tone, but surely he didn't expect her to call him Dad. Only one man had earned that right. But the fact that Nick thought she sounded like her mother made a fresh wave of grief wash over her.

"I'm sorry. I didn't recognize your voice."

"That's to be expected, I suppose." He cleared his throat. "I'm actually calling on my wife's behalf. She wondered if you might like to have dinner at our house some time next week. I realize we haven't had much time together, and…well, she thought it was the right thing to do."

Surprise washed over her. "That's very kind. I'm sure none of this has been easy on her. Maybe it would have been better if I hadn't come to London."

"No. Absolutely not. I'm glad you did. I just wish I'd known that…well, that's neither here nor there. Could you come, do you think?"

"If she's sure."

"She is. She's had a rough go of it recently, but she'd like to get to know you. As would I." Another voice sounded in the background, and Nick answered before coming back on the line. "I'd invite Luke as well, of course."

Of course. She almost smiled. Maybe he and Tiggy thought they'd need Luke's help sorting out her Southern accent. Funny how she never thought of herself as having one. But then again, no one ever thought they did. "Will you be well enough to have company? I mean, with your surgery."

"I'm a bit sore still, but, well…I don't know how long you'll be here or when you'll be back."

Kate didn't know if she'd ever be back. It all depended on how everything went. And she *had* told Luke she wanted to get to know Nick better, and possibly help with his therapy in some way. "If you're sure."

"*We* are."

She couldn't help but smile at the emphasis he'd place on the word *we*. He sounded…happy.

He didn't want to pick up his car.

Oh, some perverse part of him did, but the realist in him wanted to just call her up and say, "Keep it." His flail chest patient, despite everyone's best efforts, hadn't made it. If that wasn't bad enough, she'd evidently been a single mom, and no one knew who the baby's father was.

So the child—a little girl—was now at the mercy of the system. At least until they could find someone to give them some answers about her relatives. A social worker had already come to the hospital and carried the baby away, saying she'd get her into foster care.

And his leg hurt like the devil. The stress of running—something he normally avoided—had done a number on it. And standing for another three hours as they'd feverishly fought to stabilize the patient hadn't helped, although he'd barely noticed the throbbing pain while they'd been in the thick of battle.

The thick of battle.

There's a term he hadn't used in a while. But it was true. Emergency medicine never knew what it might face on any given day. Some days were good. And some days were horrific. Like the day he'd taken Kate by storm after losing another patient.

A day very much like today. He leaned against the hallway wall just outside the break room to take the weight off his leg.

Only he couldn't afford to let his guard down like that again. There was that little promise he'd made to Nick to consider, but it was also ridiculous to think Kate would simply fall into bed with him whenever he lost a patient—for as long as she was here, anyway.

Not only that, but he had a feeling that she was going to ask questions as soon as he saw her. She'd already looked at him oddly at the accident site, and it was doubtful he'd be able to hide the limp that went along with overdoing it. The last thing he wanted to do was trudge through old, familiar territory.

Okay, so he could take a cab over to the hotel, meet her beside his car, jump in and take off. She'd be none the wiser, right?

Unless she asked him to come up.

He didn't see that happening.

But just in case… He straightened, exhaustion taking hold as he made his way to the nurses' station. Luckily, there was a familiar face behind the desk, her dyed hair just a shade shy of blue beneath the cool light of the tube fluorescents. Mimi Copeland. His favorite nurse.

He rested a hand on the desk and waited for her to glance up at him. When she did, she gave him a compassionate smile, deep wrinkles in her cheeks coming to life. "Well, hello, Dr. Blackman. Heard you had quite a night."

"You could say that. I have to pick my car up from a

visiting…friend. Could you do me a favor and call and let her know I'm on my way?"

"You mean could I *ring* her?"

He chuckled at her good-natured ribbing, trying to ignore the speculative gleam in her eyes. *Great.* He turned a pad of paper toward himself and scribbled down the number of the hotel. "If you could ask the front desk to give Kate Bradley a message, saying I'm on my way over and could she please meet me *downstairs*." There. He'd emphasized the word. Maybe that would keep the gossip to a minimum. He doubted it, but it was the best he could do on short notice.

"Sure thing, Doctor." As she started to dial, he slowly made his way to the entrance and hailed a cab. Thankfully he didn't have to hobble much farther than the hospital entrance to find one. He'd have to wait until he got home to down a muscle relaxant, as he didn't want to drive once he'd taken it.

All the way over to the hotel he rehearsed his words, needing to keep the conversation as short as possible.

He frowned when he got there. Kate was nowhere to be seen. Maybe she was waiting inside the lobby. He handed the driver a bill, telling him to keep the change, then climbed out of the taxi, stabilizing himself on the door for a minute when his leg complained at being roused.

"Are you all right?" the taxi driver asked.

"Yep." He slammed the door, pulled in a deep breath and started walking. Parking must be underground or around back, as he didn't see anything other than a car or two in the covered check-in lane. But there was a valet booth off to the side, so maybe Kate had just left the keys with him. He could hope, anyway.

He pulled even with the guy, shifting his weight to

his good leg. "Did a Katherine Bradley leave the keys to my car with you, by any chance?"

The man's dark mustache twitched as he leaned over to check a clipboard. "Not that I can see, sir. If you have her room number I can check if you'd like."

"That's all right. I'll ask at the front desk."

Fifty feet to get inside. Fifty feet to get back out. Then the valet would bring his car round. He gritted his teeth. Once upon a time he'd run training drills with huge packs on his back and come back ready for more. Those days were long gone. Right now he could barely walk the distance it took to get inside a hotel lobby.

He knew it wasn't fair to judge things by how he felt right now. By tomorrow morning he'd probably be fine. It was the afternoons and evenings, after he'd been on his feet all day, that gave him problems.

Having to run on it…well, that was never a good idea at any time of day. Not that he'd had a choice today.

And to have his patient die anyway…thanks to a drunken idiot who hadn't known when to quit.

Like him that day in Afghanistan? No, he hadn't been drinking and, yes, he'd been trying to save one of his buddy's lives, but rushing into an unknown area was never a good idea. He'd just made himself into a target.

He pushed away the memories and schooled his face to display cool disinterest. By the time he reached the young woman manning the front desk, he was back in control. She sent him a youthful megawatt smile, which just made him feel a million years old.

"Hello. How can I help you, sir?"

He braced his hands on the desk, hoping it didn't look like he was about to leap over it and attack her. Because he wasn't. He wasn't in any shape to do much

of anything at the moment. "I'm trying to reach Kate…
er…Katherine Bradley. She's staying here."

"And you would be…?" One perfectly groomed brow
arched just a bit higher.

"Luke Blackman. Someone was supposed to leave
a message that I was picking up my car."

Why the hell wasn't Kate stepping off that elevator?

"Oh, yes, I see it. I rang Ms. Bradley right afterward
and let her know." She hesitated. "Would you like me
to try again?"

"Please." Okay, so the word hadn't come out in the
most gracious tone, so he tried again. "Thank you."

The receptionist waited, the phone pressed to her ear.
"Ms. Bradley? A Mr. Blackman is here in the lobby.
Will you be coming straight down?" She blinked a time
or two then bit her lip. "Right. Yes, I'll tell him."

She set the phone down carefully. "She's having a
bit of difficulty locating the key and wonders if you'd…
um…give her a hand."

What the…?

He stood there for a moment, trying to figure out
something that didn't involve walking, but came up
empty.

"Lift?" he gritted. Why couldn't one thing go easily today?

"Just to your left, sir."

Luke swung away from the desk and did his best
impression of a casual saunter, knowing it probably
resembled more of a duck walk. How could someone
misplace a set of keys in a hotel room? It's not like there
were a million places it could be.

He made it to the elevator and pressed the button for
the third floor, leaning against the nearest wall once he
was inside. He should have gone with his first instinct

and taken the taxi to his apartment and come back for the car tomorrow. But he had to ride right past the hotel, and had figured it would be just as easy to swing by on the way home. This was ridiculous.

When the doors opened again, he noted with relief that room 302 was just a few feet away. The door was ajar, but there was no sign of Kate. Which was good. At least she wouldn't stand there and watch him try to haul himself across the foyer. But if she expected him to be able to crawl around on his hands and knees and help search for the key, she'd be disappointed.

He knocked and the door swung open farther. "Kate?"

"Come on in. Sorry for the confusion."

When he pushed the door wider, he was shocked to find her seated in a chair, a glass of red wine in her hand, bare feet propped on the edge of the huge bed. Why was she just sitting there? Had she already located the key?

"I came to pick up my car."

"Oh, of course." She nodded at the table to her left, the slow drawl making it sound like she had all the time in the world. She was wearing some kind of stretchy pants and a loose T-shirt, like workout gear or something. "I've got the keys right here."

He drew a slow careful breath. "The receptionist said you couldn't find them."

Kate set the glass down and got to her feet, a spark of concern coming into her eyes. "Luke? How bad is it?"

He just stood there, trying to pretend he didn't hurt like a sonofabitch. He could do this. Stroll to that table, snatch the keys off it and walk back out. "I'm fine."

He took a step, forcing his leg to bear his full weight, and almost lost it. Sweat broke out on his forehead as he took a second and then a third step, his jaw working hard to contain the flurry of evil words that were swirling in his head.

"Stop it!" She grabbed the keys and moved in front of him. "I'm so sorry. I had no idea you'd be in this much pain."

"I don't know what you mean."

"I talked to Nick this evening, but I never imagined…"

His eyes closed. Of course she'd talked to him. He'd seen the way she'd looked at his leg at the accident scene. If she was truly a physical therapist, she could decode the signals, just like all the other therapists who'd worked on him. And none of them had done him a lick of good.

He knew that wasn't a fair assessment. They were the reason he was able to walk at all. But he wasn't walking. Not really. He was hobbling. He could put on a pretty good show for as long as it took him to get off work. But it cost him. Each and every damn day.

"Great. You talked to him. You know all my dirty little secrets." He held out his hand. "So give me the keys, and I'll get out of your hair."

"Sure. On one condition." She walked back to the side table, curvy hips bumping in a smooth, steady rhythm as she picked up a glass of water and two tablets sitting next to it. That didn't matter right now, though. Nothing did, except getting those keys, taking three steps out of the room and somehow reaching his car.

"The condition is that you tell me about how things went with your patient…while I work on your leg."

CHAPTER SIX

SHE WAITED FOR the explosion she was sure would come, but there was none.

Instead, Luke pivoted on his good foot and sat on the edge of the bed. "I'm too tired to play this game with you right now, Kate. Please, just give me the keys."

"I'm not playing games. Nick said you'd been injured during your time in the service. Don't worry, he didn't give me all the gory details. But I can tell your leg hurts. It's been hurting ever since the accident, it's bothering you enough that you're having trouble walking across the room to pick up a set of keys. How safe is it for you to drive when it's like this?"

"Safe enough."

Okay, she probably should have met him downstairs like he'd asked, but she'd had no idea he'd be in such agony. And he wouldn't dream of coming out and admitting he was in pain. She'd had enough difficult patients to know when one was minimizing his problem, trying to keep it under wraps.

She set the glass, along with his keys and pills, on the dresser, then knelt next to the bed. "I have a heating pad, and I brought a few of my tools from home, in case I decided to…" She'd been about to say *"stay for a while,"* but it didn't seem appropriate to mention that right now. She didn't want there to be any kind of misunderstanding between them. She wasn't trying to start anything, but it had made her chest ache to see him try to hurry on that roadway today. He probably hadn't even realized she'd seen him.

"I just need to get some rest. It'll be fine by morning."

"I don't believe you."

He shut his eyes for a second, a muscle working in his jaw, before he fixed her with an angry glare. "No? Well, lady, I don't give a damn what you believe. I didn't seem to have any trouble lifting you onto that sink, did I? So give me my damn keys and let me get out of here."

Okay, that hurt. More than hurt. She clenched her jaw as angry words whisked up her airway and tumbled into her mouth, beating against the backs of her teeth in an effort to get out.

This has nothing to do with you, Kate, and everything to do with Luke trying to protect himself.

She'd had men like him cross her treatment table before. Military types who hated admitting weakness and hated it even worse when Kate focused all her attention on that weakness—which was what she had to do in order to help them. She was charged with manipulating the very spot, knowing the injury was as much a source of mental anguish as it was physical. And sometimes facing their own mortality day in and day out was more painful than anything else.

"No, you didn't have any trouble. But I should have noticed something was wrong even then."

"And if you had? Would it have made a difference?" The challenge was unmistakable.

Would she have still let him do what he had?

Definitely. It didn't make him any less attractive.

"No, it wouldn't have made any difference."

Admitting it made what they'd done seem that much worse, for some reason. Her patients were usually in a vulnerable place when she saw them. She would never dream of taking advantage of that.

But Luke *wasn't* her patient. She hadn't known about his injury at the time—he'd hidden it well. And he sure as hell hadn't been the picture of vulnerability. Then or now.

Because he was good at hiding his weakness.

But not nearly as good as her mother—who'd almost taken her secrets to the grave.

She pushed that thought aside. It had nothing to do with what would or wouldn't happen in this room. If Luke stood and demanded his keys, she'd give them to him and let him walk away. And she'd walk away, too. He'd talked about being too tired to play this game. Well, so was she. She was hurting inside, just like he was, even if it was for a completely different reason. And she wasn't sure if she could manage her pain *and* his right now.

All she wanted to do was ease a little of his hurt. Nothing more. And doing so would take her mind off her own problems. Off the fact that she still didn't know how she was going to deal with her newfound knowledge or what Nick's place would be in her life.

Or if she even wanted him to have a place.

She sucked in a deep breath and stood. "Come on, Luke. Surely it can't hurt to have me work on it a little bit. You can just think of it as getting a free massage."

A free massage.

Unfortunately that was not what he was thinking of at all, but he wasn't quite sure how he was going to get out of this room. His physical therapist had once told him he should use a cane, but he'd refused to go there. And most days he got along just fine without one.

It was only when he strained the damaged muscles beyond their limits that they gave him trouble. And when they rebelled, they went all out. The muscles were currently bunched in an angry ball at the top of his thigh. Forcing them to keep on working just made the knot tighten further.

A muscle relaxant would help, but it would take hours to take effect, and he'd still have a devil of a time getting to sleep tonight. And he was due at work first thing in the morning.

He wasn't sure he wanted Kate's hands on him right now, though. Not after what had happened between them before.

She hadn't bothered to wait for his response but was busy setting various items on the bed.

What could it hurt? If he embarrassed himself, it wasn't like she was going to be around to remind him of it. And he was dog tired. The last thing he wanted to do was stand up and somehow make his way back down to the car. His leg was going to fight him every step of the way.

"Where do you want me?"

Her fingers paused on a towel that she was rolling into a tight tube. "I'll lay a blanket on the floor. The bed is too soft."

She went to the closet, pulled a heavy brown blanket from the top shelf and folded it into a pallet, placing it at the foot of the bed. "Take your shoes and pants off, please."

Pants? Oh, hell, no.

"I'd rather keep them on, if it's all the same to you."

"Your shoes?"

He gave her a tight smile. "I think you know what I mean."

"I have to really knead those muscles, and to do that, I need to see what I'm working with."

His joking comment to Nick—asking if he wanted him to drop his pants and show Kate his handiwork—came back to taunt him. Yeah, well, he'd never expected to have to drop them...literally. And he wasn't all that thrilled with the idea of her seeing the ugly network of scars and divots where there should be a smooth layer of skin over muscle.

She stopped organizing stuff and looked up at him. "I'll put a towel over you. Besides, it's not like you'll be naked or anything."

He hadn't been naked that time in the supply closet either, but that hadn't stopped him from pulling her hips against him and sinking deep.

Yeah, something he'd better stop thinking about. Now.

Instead, he concentrated on the ache in his leg and the exhaustion that made him want to fall back onto the bed and ride out the pain with his eyes closed. He wouldn't be able to sleep, but he could at least stop thinking about things that didn't revolve around pain.

"How long will this take?"

"Around a half hour."

Surely he could survive that length of time.

"I want the towel first."

"Of course." She lifted a decent-sized bath towel. "I've got it right here."

Since the principal injury was at the top of his leg and hip—the explosion had damn near blown his balls off—that should cover the worst of his wound. She'd only need to see the scars that ran down the top of his thigh, where the shredded muscle fibers had been painstakingly stitched back together.

He was damned if he was going to undress in front of her, though. So he grabbed the towel from between her fingers and made his way—step by painful step—into the bathroom, where he proceeded to toe off his loafers and unzip his slacks. He didn't try to bend down and pull them off, he just let them slide down his legs, avoiding the mirror.

It seemed pretty stupid to worry about aesthetics in the face of everything else he had to worry about. But if he didn't look, he could avoid remembering the sudden searing pain that had ripped the breath from his lungs and the weakness that had stolen over him as his lifeblood had seeped from his body.

Flattening a hand on the vanity top, he supported part of his weight as he stepped out of the slacks. He then wrapped the towel tightly around his midsection and secured the loose end, thankful it hung almost to his knees.

There. That should do it.

He limped back into the room, the sound of elevator music coming from the television speakers.

Great. She was determined to really play this therapist thing to the hilt, wasn't she?

Kate patted the blanket, where she'd already laid out a pillow. "Let's put you on your back, head up here."

Holding the edges of the towel together with one hand and putting his other on the edge of the bed, he somehow managed to lower himself without falling. He stretched out, and just the act of being off that leg was heavenly. It still hurt, but now it was just a deep ache that went in through his skin and bored through all the layers before anchoring itself in his bone.

"Sit up for a second."

Once he did, she handed him a couple of pills and a glass of water.

He glanced at the pills. Ibuprofen. He lifted his brows. "Really?" He'd been planning on taking something a hell of a lot stronger when he got home.

"They'll help with the inflammation and at least take the edge off the pain. Hopefully by the time you're ready to leave."

"I know what they do."

"Oh." She colored. "Of course you do. Sorry. I don't have anything stronger."

He tossed the pills into his mouth and downed them with a long swig of icy water. He kept drinking until the glass was empty. "Thanks."

She took it from him. "You're welcome."

"You really don't have to do this."

"I know. But I want to." She nodded toward the pillow. "Lie back."

She slid the towel she'd rolled earlier beneath the knee of his injured leg to support it.

So far, so good.

The second she pushed the towel up, however, and he felt the first splash of warm oil hit his skin, Luke knew he'd made a terrible mistake.

CHAPTER SEVEN

THE SCARS WERE everywhere. And she had a feeling she hadn't even seen the worst of them.

Kate swallowed back her horror as she smoothed the massage oil across his skin.

From beneath the towel a deep concave groove appeared, which branched into a spider web of smaller scars, the whole tangled mess stopping just before it reached his knee. Two square patches of skin appeared to have been slapped over a portion of his leg, one of them longer than the other, disappearing beneath the lower edge of the towel.

Skin grafts.

Where had they harvested them from?

Probably the back of his hip.

Luke's other leg was untouched. Smooth skin over strong muscles. His good leg had taken up the slack during the healing process, growing stronger even as the injured leg grew weaker. There was a size differential that was unmistakable.

When she glanced at his face, she saw his eyes were shut, long, curling lashes appearing at odds with the fierce lines of his cheekbones. He probably hated knowing she was looking at the damage—wondering if she was disgusted by the sight.

Not at all.

But she did feel a deep sadness at what had happened to him. She knew soldiers every day were struck down in the prime of their lives. Luke was lucky to be alive. And if she wasn't mistaken, he was very lucky to still have this leg. The damage had been extensive. Whoever had repaired it had done a good job. Nick? Not likely. It looked to be the work of more than one specialist. But he'd mentioned Nick saving his life, so he'd been involved somehow.

She pulled her mind back to the job at hand. "This is going to hurt at first, but it should start feeling better as things loosen up."

"I'll be fine." Even as he said it, the muscles in his leg contracted as if undergoing an assault. And really it was. But it needed to be done.

She wouldn't dig in deep right away. She'd slowly work her way up to the hard stuff.

An unwilling smile tugged her lips.

Laying her hands on his leg, she started to massage, using long silky strokes that had little therapeutic value. It was really just a ploy to make his muscles think she wasn't going to go after them. As if by magic, the tension in his leg began to ease. She kept at it, discreetly edging the towel higher and higher, trying to do it without him noticing. Not because she wanted to sneak a peek, but because she had a feeling the worst of the damage was yet to come. She was right. More grafting. Furrows where skin should have overlaid muscle. It looked like he'd lost some actual muscle tissue. No wonder the leg was weak. It was a wonder he was walking as well as he was.

A low huff of air escaped his lungs, making her smile widen. He was determined to make her work for this, wasn't he? Well, he'd find she could be pretty stubborn herself. She wanted to get just one satisfied groan out of him.

She also needed to get her mind out of the gutter. She'd never had a patient affect her like this.

Because he *wasn't* her patient. And why did she feel the need to keep reminding herself of that fact? Maybe because she'd never worked on anyone she'd had sex with before.

Her strokes got firmer, but still not hard enough to make him wince. She stopped to pour a little more oil on her hands, letting it dribble onto his leg.

"The hotel's not going to be very happy if you get that stuff on their blanket," he said.

"It's water soluble. I'll take it down and ask them to clean it tomorrow. No biggie."

"Water soluble? As in…?"

Leave it to a doctor to understand the implications. "Don't worry, I'm not using *that* jelly on you."

His lips quirked, one eye opening to glance at her. "No need to, from what I remember."

Egads. Heat splashed hot and fast into her face. The man sure wasn't burdened by many inhibitions, was he?

Her best bet was to ignore that remark. "I want to get a couple of warm towels to put on your leg. Be right back."

She turned the hot tap on in the bathroom and reached to get a hand towel from the chrome fixture above the toilet. Her eyes met their reflection in the mirror, and she shook her head when she noted her face was as pink as she'd feared. If they were going to talk, she needed to direct the conversation and keep it in the shallow end of the pool.

Testing the water with her fingers, she refolded the

towel into a rectangle that would fit over the muscles just above his knee. The towel would help loosen those while she worked on the upper ones. She could reverse it later on.

She slid the towel beneath the flow of hot water and wet it enough to be effective, but not so much that it was dripping. She then switched on the heating rack on the wall and let it work on the bath towels already draped over it.

"Kate?"

"Coming." She hurried into the other room and knelt beside him again, sliding the towel into place and letting the moist heat soak deep into his muscles.

He groaned.

Success!

She worked for a few minutes, casting around for some innocuous topic of conversation. But Luke seemed pretty happy just to lie there for now, so maybe there was no need to talk. And judging from the twitch she'd just spotted behind that towel, he was struggling to keep his mind off how close she was getting to certain areas of his body.

Afraid he might leap up and demand to leave before she'd finished, she eased away and headed back down toward the center of his thigh.

A little more muscle went into the next wave of strokes as Kate tried to isolate muscle groups and loosen the thick adhesions caused by the scarring process. This was where things got serious, and in the same way her manipulation of his leg became more aggressive, so did Luke's demeanor. Not that he lashed out verbally, like he had earlier, but the bulge behind his towel subsided, and a muscle in his cheek began to pulse, letting her know he was struggling to deal with the discomfort. But he stayed put. It was probably a matter of pride more than anything else right now.

He may be a doctor by profession, but at his core he was still a tough military guy. Don't give quarter, don't show pain.

She stopped twice to replace the cooling towel with a fresh hot one, and shifted her attention to the lower section of his thigh, hoping to draw the pain down and out of his body. This area was less damaged than the upper portion and evidently less sensitive as well, because Luke relaxed the second she slid the warm towel up to cover the part on which she'd already worked. She sensed his relief that she was moving away from that area.

She reapplied the oil to her palms, noting they were pink from the work. But it felt good to be back in her element, helping someone who needed it. And it was helping her as well, keeping her mind off her current problems.

"Remember I told you about researching some of the UK hospitals that offer LSVT therapy?"

He grunted in response, and Kate wasn't sure that was an affirmation or not. So she kept going. "Your hospital offers it. Did you know that?"

She paused, glancing up to see his eyes had opened a bit and he was now regarding her with what looked like suspicion. Maybe he thought she was going to press him about helping with Nick. She'd still like to, if he needed it, but what she'd really love would be to observe how another therapy center operated. Maybe even work there for a bit while she was here, even if on a volunteer basis. Being cooped up in her hotel room day in and day out didn't appeal to her. And she didn't feel right inviting herself over to Nick and Tiggy's house.

Maybe Luke would be willing to put in a good word for her at the center.

"Anyway, I was thinking." She put her hands back on his leg and focused on massaging while she got to the point. "Maybe you could introduce me around and ask if I could observe their techniques."

No response. She sneaked another glance at his face. His eyes were closed again and that telltale muscle was working in his jaw. Surely she wasn't hurting him now. Her fingers were barely making any indentations in his skin.

"Luke, are you awake?"

"Oh, yeah. Wide awake."

His tone was odd, as well. She glanced at the towel, thinking maybe he was talking about what was behind it, but it was as still as death.

She swallowed, but forged ahead. "So what do you think?"

"Is that what this was all about?"

This? This what?

"I'm not sure what you mean."

"Were you trying to get an 'in' with the hospital in the same way you were trying to get an 'in' with Nick's treatment?"

"No, of course not." Outrage crowded her chest. She'd been trying to help him, and he was thinking she'd only done it to get something she wanted? "I miss my job, that's all. I was just sitting here thinking about how much I love doing this. How good it feels to watch your muscles relax as my hands slide over them. How good it feels to have…"

Oh, my. The towel wasn't so still anymore. In fact, it was—

"How good it feels to what, Kate?" His voice rumbled through her senses about the same time as he slowly lifted his body into a sitting position. Since she'd been kneeling over his leg, that put them nose to nose. A potent combination of anger and something even more powerful glittered in his eyes.

His hand slid around the back of her neck, keeping her from moving away.

"I—I was talking about work," she whispered, warm liquid anticipation beginning to flow through her veins, despite her words.

"Were you?" His thumb slid down her jaw until it hooked beneath her chin, tilting it up slightly. "I was talking about...this."

With that, his lips closed the narrow gap between them and slid over hers.

CHAPTER EIGHT

HER HANDS WERE still on his leg.

Moisture from the towel draped over his upper thigh seeped through the dry one around his waist, but he didn't care. He'd done so well controlling his urges during that crazy massage. Well, during most of it, anyway. When that control had started to slip and his body had responded despite every effort he'd made to think of other things, Kate had seemed to know exactly what to do to help him regain it. She had clamped down on his leg and gone to town, drowning out any sensation other than acute discomfort. The pain had been welcome, though.

He waited for her to repeat the action and help him switch his body off again.

She didn't. Her hands just kept resting lightly on his thigh, even as her mouth began to return the pressure as it opened. Then her hands were off his leg and around his neck.

She'd had to go and ask that damn question. The one that had made him question her motives all over again. Because the second she had, he'd forgotten all about the pain. Or maybe that was the ibuprofen.

Right now he didn't care what had caused him to snap. Because kissing her lips had been all he'd thought about for the past three days. That and those sexy little sighs as he'd taken her.

Hell, he couldn't do this. Nick was counting on him to keep it in his pants.

Only his pants were long gone. And his leg was feeling better by the minute. Probably because every ounce of blood was rushing to the founding member of the do-something-stupid-now club.

But Nick...

Her fingers slid into his hair, sending shock waves rolling through his entire body.

Who cared what Nick thought, anyway? This woman had the ability to cut off all brain function that didn't involve getting her into a prone position as fast as possible.

No. Not fast. He'd already had the slam-bam experience with her, and it had rocked his world. So slow and easy would probably blow it to smithereens.

She whimpered and pressed closer, and he realized her mouth was still open, still inviting. Well, far be it for him to disappoint a lady. Wrapping one hand around her waist, he hauled her closer, swiveling her so her knees were beside his left hip.

The act tipped her sideways onto his chest, which was about as close as he dared get to pulling her onto his lap, which was where he really wanted her. He had enough sense, though, to know that was a recipe for disaster. And not just because of his leg.

Speaking of legs, still kissing her, he tossed the damp towel she'd used during the massage to the side and buried a hand in her hair, which was loose around her shoulders. God, it was so incredibly soft. Just like her mouth, which was drawing him deeper, urging him to take what he wanted.

And he would. Very soon.

Leaving her mouth, he pressed slow biting kisses inch by inch along her jaw, drawing a moan from her throat that went straight to his groin.

"I'm supposed to be taking care of your leg," she whispered.

He lifted his head, that drawl of hers singing through his head. "The leg's all better. Now it's my turn to take care of you."

"Oh."

He smiled. His hand skimmed beneath her T-shirt and found that skin he'd been craving, his fingers splaying over her back, thumb gliding in a back and forth arc over her hip. "How are your knees feeling?"

Her eyes widened. "M-my knees?"

Her skin turned deliciously pink and he lifted a hand, drawing his fingers along the line of her cheek. "You've been kneeling a while, and I thought it might be uncomfortable."

Kate wrinkled her nose and slid down until she was resting on her left hip. Her glance went to his towel, which appeared to be levitating. "I don't think you need to worry about your modesty anymore, do you?" Her fingers went to the tucked-in portion, and he moved to stop her before it was too late.

"Don't." The word was a harsh command, and she blinked up at him, surprise written across her face. He nodded toward the overhead light, forcing his voice to soften. "Can you turn that off?"

Kate tilted her head, her hands still gripping the edge of his towel. Turn off the light. Right now? She wouldn't be able to see him if she...

Oh. She got it. The towel had nothing to do with

modesty and everything to do with the condition of his leg. He didn't want her to see it. "Luke, I've already seen your leg. Touched it. It's okay. Really."

She leaned over and tasted his lips, nibbled across them, something inside of her aching over his request. Had he made all of his dates since the accident dim the lights before they were intimate?

At first she thought he was going to lean back and withdraw, or continue to insist that the lights go off, but then he grabbed her to him—fast enough that it took her breath away. His mouth slanted over hers, and if she thought he'd been kissing her before, she had been wrong. Hard lips held hers prisoner, forcing them apart and burying his tongue in the depths of her mouth.

He held her against him, her breasts flattening against his chest as he continued to take her mouth with long, hard strokes. A small sound exited her throat as she wound her arms around his head and held him close, trying to bind them together.

His head canted sideways as if needing to explore her from every angle, his mouth dragging across hers before settling back in and starting the sequence all over again.

This man was all muscle and sinew…and hot, heady need.

He drew back enough to whisper against her mouth. "There's a condom in my wallet in the bathroom."

"I'll get it." She knew exactly why he'd muttered it. He couldn't get up and walk to the bathroom. Not yet. Not with his leg the way it was. Oh, how that admission must have cost him. She'd just uncurled her legs and stood when a tug at her waistband stopped her. She turned back round, surprised when his fingers undid the button on her slacks and drew down the zipper.

She swallowed as he tugged her closer, still parting

the fabric and using the edges to slide them over her hips and down her calves.

"Step out of them."

She did as he asked, standing there in her white lace panties. Was he going to repeat his actions from the supply closet and yank them off her? No. Instead, he tunneled beneath the elastic of the legs, his hands curving up and over her butt. She expected him to squeeze her cheeks and feel her up—and she'd have been happy to let him but no. He used his grip to urge her toward him. When she hesitated, his mouth curved in that crazy half grin. "Come here, Kate."

She gulped, but allowed him to draw her closer until he was right there. *Right* there. Pressed against her. He opened his mouth and surrounded her, biting down with enough pressure to make her gasp. Then his tongue slid over her in one hot, wet swipe, the heat traveling right through the fabric. Her eyes shuddered closed, wanting more. Now. Just as her hips edged closer, he backed off, his hands sliding free of her panties. When she blinked down at him in confusion, he flashed another knowing smile. "My wallet is in the back pocket of my pants."

She stood paralyzed for a second or two, before her mind absorbed what he'd said. He wanted her to walk to the bathroom.

Lordy, he'd just set her body on fire, and the man knew it. She swiveled to the left, her legs a bit unsteady as they carried her toward the bathroom. With each step she felt his eyes on her, the place between her legs already pulsing with need. She'd been on the verge of exploding, and he'd barely even touched her.

And when he did?

She found his pants on the floor and picked them up, sliding her hand into the back pocket and retrieving his wallet. She flipped it open, and rummaged around before finding the compartment with the packet inside. Make that *two* packets. Hmm… Just in case, she removed both of them and headed back to the bedroom.

When she got there, the lights were off, and she squinted at the pallet, only to find it empty. For a second she thought he might have taken off, but then she remembered him asking her to turn out the lights. She'd refused, so he'd found a way to do it, anyway. So where was he? As if he'd read her thoughts, he called, "Over here."

Peering through the darkness, she could barely make out his form on the bed. Back leaning against the headboard, long legs stretched out in front of him.

She licked her lips. "Found them."

She knew why he'd asked her to get his wallet but why had he gotten on the bed while she'd been in the bathroom, instead of waiting for her to return?

He hadn't wanted her to see him struggle to walk, if his leg was still bothering him. So he'd done it quickly, while she'd been out of the room. Her heart cramped further. She ignored it. The last thing he'd want was for her to make a comment or try to reassure him.

Instead, she tossed the condoms onto the bed, hoping they landed somewhere near his left side. Then she crawled slowly toward him, her eyes beginning to adjust to the gloom. If she was on top, he wouldn't have to worry about his leg. When she reached him, she kissed his lips then put her plan into action, swinging her leg over his hips, straddling him— Oh…he was naked! And hard. Gloriously hard.

This was good.

Still pressing her mouth to his, her breasts flattened against his chest. The heat of his body burned against her most private place, making her squirm. *Mmm.* When he muttered something against her mouth, she wiggled again, feeling a definite response from him this time. So she repeated the act, sliding slowly along his naked length. There was definitely something to be said for being in charge of a man like this.

And men liked it, too, right? When the woman took the lead?

She leaned up onto her elbows and smoothed his hair back from his forehead.

"What do you think you're doing?" There was dark humor lacing his voice.

"Playing with your hair."

"No. I mean here." He pressed up with his hips, rubbing against her in a way that made her gasp. "What are you doing here?"

"I thought I'd be on top." She pressed a kiss to his throat then licked halfway to his chin. She was startled when all of a sudden she was flipped flat onto her back, where she landed with an *"Oomph."*

"You thought wrong." Her breath sawed in and out of her lungs at the dark, hungry look she could just make out in his eyes. "You think I can't do this?"

He pressed into her in a way that said, yes, he could, in fact. His voice lowered further. "I can. And I will. Very soon." His teeth grazed her cheek. "You can be on top next time."

All she heard were the words *very soon* and *next time*.

Then his mouth was on hers and he was kissing her until her head spun.

Next time? Oh, Lord, so he'd taken those two condoms at face value. They were going to have more than one session tonight. And next time she was going to be on top.

All she could think of was that maybe she should call the front desk and tell them to hold all her calls.

He sat up, straddling her hips in much the way she'd straddled his. Her hands went to his waist and started to slide lower, meaning to touch him. He stopped her. "Next time."

Not fair. But she wasn't about to argue.

Then his hands were on her shirt, and he tugged it up and over her head, letting it drop beside the bed. His palms curved over her breasts, molding them to his hands. Sweet desire pumped through her veins, and she arched into his touch. His fingers left their perch and glided from her collarbone, down over her breasts, grazing her nipples as they passed and then continued down her belly.

He swirled a lazy fingertip into her belly button, his thumb running along the elastic on her panties, then beneath it, traveling over the fine hairs until he'd reached her center. He moved lower, pushing inside, the same way his tongue had pushed inside her mouth a few minutes earlier.

She whimpered as the rest of his hand curved over that most sensitive part of her. He stroked in and out a couple of times, while she tried to lift her hips to meet him. He stilled.

"Rip open one of the condoms."

All she wanted to do was lie there and absorb the heady sensations caused by the continued intimate contact, but she dutifully fumbled her hand across the surface of the bed until she found the nearest condom.

It took several tries before she finally located the nick

in the side and tore the packaging. Luke rewarded her with a couple more easy glides of his thumb.

God, that felt good. Too good. Her fingers stopped what they were doing as her eyes fluttered shut. She needed to push against him. But couldn't because his weight was still on top of her.

"Take it out."

He had to be kidding. She could barely think, much less do anything requiring a co-ordinated plan of attack. "I—I…"

His thumb slowly withdrew, the pressure of the rest of his hand on her fading with each lost millimeter.

"Luke…" She squirmed. "Please."

"Take it out of the package, Kate."

Oh, that was mean. But her fingers somehow slid into the opening and found the condom, managing to wrestle it free.

As soon as she did, his hand was over hers, guiding her, before moving to grip himself by the base and letting her slowly unroll the condom over his length. Their fingers met in the middle. He joined her in finishing the process and the mingling of their hands on his flesh was heady.

He wrapped his hand around hers, using her fingers to slowly stroke himself over and over.

God. He was too much. She'd thought he'd been erotic in the supply closet. This was light years beyond that.

He finally released her and dragged his thumb across her lower lip, his other still lodged inside her body. "I don't think we're going to need any of your massage oil."

Her face heated as he withdrew his hand and slowly leaned over her, until his lips were at her ear. "I love it that you're so wet. So ready." He moved up over her hips, biting her earlobe. "Spread your legs for me, Kate."

She'd never had a man mutter words like this to her. Ever. And if he'd ordered her around in any other tone of voice, she'd have told him where to stick it. But his voice was low, mellow, rumbled directly against her ear and sent delicious shivers through her body. It was a complete turn-on and totally different from what she'd experienced in the past. He voiced his wishes and expected her to obey.

And hell if she didn't.

Her thighs parted, and Luke slid between them, his legs pressing against hers to hold them in place. She felt his fingers at the crotch of her panties, tugging them to one side, his penis finding her. He eased just inside, then withdrew, her moisture making each pass a little smoother. His breath shuddered against her cheek as he suddenly pushed completely inside her, stretching and filling her, and her muscles clenched around him in reaction.

"Holy hell."

She echoed that sentiment. Whew. He felt as good on a bed as he had on a sink. No, better, because there something incredibly intimate about having a man press you into a mattress.

She was glad she wasn't on top.

Sliding her palms down the smooth skin of his back, she tried to memorize the lusciousness of his warmth against her. She was still in her bra and panties, and there was no hint that he was in a hurry to remove either garment. That drove her crazy, as well. In fact, everything about this man did.

He withdrew only to thrust into her again, deeper this time, drawing a strangled moan from her as she strained upward, wanting to get closer. Keeping himself buried inside her, he lifted onto his elbows and kissed her lips, her collarbone, the top of her breast, before his mouth closed over the fabric-covered peak.

Holy hell. She didn't voice the words like he had, but they sang through her head over and over as he drew her nipple further into his mouth, the friction of the wet fabric over her sensitive flesh taking her higher. She wasn't far.

"Luke," she whispered, her shaking hands coming up to cradle his head against her as his tongue rubbed back and forth over her. The sensation went straight to her center, where her flesh tightened around his again.

Move. Please.

He did. Withdrawing just enough to put some space between them.

No!

When he kept tugging on her nipple, making no move to set up any kind of rhythm down below, she grew desperate. She lifted her hips in an effort to relieve some of the ache between her legs then backed away, rising to repeat the act as his breathing deepened, rattling against her chest.

She realized what he was doing. Holding still and forcing her to ride him as she might have done had she been on top. And so she did. Luke rewarded each strong pump of her hips with a long slow lap of his tongue before moving to the other breast, the agonizing vortex he was creating sucking her a little deeper with each stroke.

His knees were flat on the bed and so she hooked her feet around them in an effort to gain more leverage, pushing up hard, until the sensitive bead of flesh at the joint of her thighs finally connected with his pelvis.

Oh! Yes. That.

She mashed closer, holding herself high against him and rubbing in little circles, her legs shaking with exertion but needing this so very badly. She pressed her hands low on his back, using her arms to keep that precious line of connection.

Please. Oh, God. Just a little bit more.

Her legs started to fail her, and she lunged back up in desperation, forcing her body to slide against his over and over...

Ahhhh!

She went off, her body convulsing around him as she fell back to the bed. He followed her down, suddenly thrusting into her at a wild pace, releasing her breast and throwing his head back. The cords on his neck stood out and a growl erupted from his chest as he seated himself deep, deep within her, holding himself there for what seemed like forever.

When he settled back against her, his head dropped to her neck, breath gusting against her moist skin. An aftershock went through her, and her flesh clamped down on him again. He responded by pressing closer.

"Mmm." The contented sound came from somewhere down around her shoulder, punctuated with a small bite at the joint. The shot arced straight down her spinal cord, and she squeezed tight again. He paused, then repeated the act to the same effect. "I think somebody likes that."

She liked just about anything he did. She groaned, half amused, half embarrassed by what he made her body do.

He lifted his head and smiled down at her. "Look on the bright side, Kate. At least you didn't lose your panties this time."

CHAPTER NINE

THE PHYSICAL THERAPIST set aside her butcher's knife and pulled a protective silicone stump sleeve from a huge drawer filled with prosthetics of every imaginable size and shape—arms, legs, the bottom portion of a face— and held it up. "This looks to be the right size."

Luke glanced at the bed next to his where a young amputee had been brought in earlier today. It was now empty. So was the bed to his right. He frowned. Then who was the sleeve for?

Horror gripped him as he slowly dragged the sheet covering the lower half of his body away from his legs. The left one was fine. Strong. Whole. The right one...

The bloody bandages that had once covered his leg were now lying flat against the bed, still wound around and around, as if his leg had simply vanished into thin air, leaving behind the empty wrappings. And the therapist's face, observing him with a secretive smile, came into sudden focus as she leaned toward him.

Kate.

What had she done to him?

He screamed...

"Luke." The sound came from beside him, along with a hand gripping his arm. Shaking him.

He jerked away from the touch, blinking as reality returned.

She leaned toward him just like before, only the smirk was gone. In its place was worry, her brows drawn together as she reached for him again.

"Luke? Are you okay?"

He fell back against the pillows, flexing his right leg. Still there. It was a dream.

Bloody hell, he was drenched with sweat. The last thing he wanted was for her to see him like this. He made to get up, only to have her stop him.

"Hey. What's going on?"

If he started suddenly yanking his clothes on, he had a feeling she'd follow him, pestering him with questions.

"Bad dream, I guess."

"I guess so. Are you okay?"

He dragged a hand through his hair, pushing it off his brow and ignoring her repeated question. "What time is it?"

"Just after eight in the morning. Sorry, I guess I fell asleep."

Kate was sitting with the sheet pulled up around her breasts—breasts that were now completely bare. Her blond hair was gloriously tousled, her eyes soft with sleep, but he couldn't banish the image of her tucking that huge knife out of sight. That strange, secretive smile. Maybe his subconscious couldn't separate the physical pain he'd endured last night from the pleasure she'd given him. She'd hurt him and then helped him. Just like in his dream.

"We both fell asleep." Maybe it was a good thing he'd had that dream. He needed something to knock some sense into his head. What he'd done last night had been crazy. And if Nick found out, he was going to kill him. "I need to get to work, though. My shift starts in a little over an hour."

"How's your leg?"

He jerked his glance to her face before he realized she wasn't talking about his dream but about the massage. He stretched it again, surprised that the muscles seemed to have recovered from the abuse he'd put them through at the accident scene. "All better. Thanks."

He put his feet over the side of the bed, keeping the sheet pulled over his thighs. He'd never thought to check last night to make sure the curtains were pulled all the way shut. They weren't, and daylight was pouring into the room through the gap between them.

"Um, Luke?"

He twisted to look at her, waiting for her to continue.

"Have you thought about what I asked? About the therapy center at the hospital?"

"No." All his misgivings from yesterday came rushing back. Along with all of his suspicions. "Have you talked to Nick about this?"

"Not yet. But I was planning on saying something soon."

"I think he's almost done with his physical therapy course. At least, that's what I understood. I'm supposed to meet him at the center when I get in today."

The hand Kate was using to hold the sheet curled until she was clenching it against herself. "Oh. I didn't realize he was almost finished with his treatment…"

Last night had been a mistake. The last thing he wanted to do was get involved in Nick's business. Especially since he couldn't seem to keep his hands off that "business."

"Like I said, you can talk to him about it."

"I'd still like to observe, even if Nick isn't there any more. I can learn so much from seeing other approaches."

Did he really want to have this discussion this morning? "I can't promise anything. But I'll check and see if they allow that kind of thing."

She leaned over and kissed him on the cheek. "Thank you."

He climbed out of bed, still feeling a little queasy from the dream he'd had. Maybe it really *was* his subconscious; maybe it was trying to give him a warning kick in the ass. He kept his leg angled where she couldn't see it. "Listen. This—" he motioned at the bed "—can't happen again."

Her eyes widened with hurt, and then her teeth came down on her lip. "Of course. I, um, feel the same way. I'm not going to be here for that long, anyway."

"Okay, then. As long as we're on the same page." He grabbed the rest of his clothes and headed for the bathroom. Why did he feel like such a schmuck? He'd just done what needed doing. Nick would not be happy about him spending the night here. Not that he planned on breathing a word of this to anyone. One slip-up was understandable—after all, Kate was a beautiful woman—but two? Not his usual style.

Especially not after displaying the kind of weakness he'd shown last night.

Hell, as erotic as it had been to make her set the pace, to force her to push up into him over and over, it had served a dual purpose. He'd been having a tough time getting the muscles in his weak leg to cooperate during the act. His pride had been stung when she'd climbed on top, and so he'd thought he'd show her that he was as good as the next guy.

Only he wasn't. He couldn't even make love to a woman without having to worry about his goddamned leg giving out in the middle of it.

He sat on the lid of the commode and dragged both his hands through his hair. Staring down at his leg and the mangled flesh and skin grafts that stretched from his right hip to his knee, he winced. He couldn't even stand to have a woman look at him. It was lights out, all the way.

Kate had undoubtedly seen quite a bit of the damage during the massage, but not all of it. And certainly not the stuff on the inside.

He stood and yanked on his briefs, letting the elastic waistband snap against his skin.

"Where'd you get the scar?" Her voice came from the other side of the door.

Was she kidding him? Scar…singular? He stepped into his slacks, zipping them up and fastening the button. "I already told you."

"No, not your leg. The one on your chest. Near your tattoo."

He glanced in the mirror at his other war wound. From a completely different war—and one that didn't bother him nearly as much. That one had been fought on the streets of Chicago in back of a bar—over a woman, of all things. He'd allowed himself to be goaded into going into the alley to fight, only to have the other guy pull a knife on him. He'd seen the metallic glint just as it had come toward him—too late to duck away.

The slice hadn't been terribly deep, but it had almost bisected his left nipple and stretched halfway down his stomach, where it was inches away from meeting up with his other wound. He'd been a drunken fool. Way too young to have gotten into a situation like that.

And it had sealed his decision to go into the military, as his father had basically disowned him that night. As soon as the stitches had come out, he'd gone to the nearest recruitment center and signed on the dotted line. The tattoo of an eagle on his left shoulder had come later, after he'd graduated from boot camp.

Funny how that scar didn't carry the same baggage as the other one. And he didn't mind anyone seeing that one. He rubbed his chest. "I got it in a bar fight."

There was silence for a second. Then her voice came back through. "Really? Was that before or after your leg injury?"

He doubted the outcome would have been quite the same if the fight had happened afterward. The other guy had wound up with a broken nose and a pair of black eyes once he'd kicked the knife out of his hand.

No kicking anything out of anyone's hand nowadays. "Before. I was young and stupid."

So what was his excuse now?

"Are you almost done? I need the bathroom."

He dragged his shirt on over his head and opened the door. "It's all yours. Listen, I'll see myself out."

"I hate to ask, but would you mind giving me a lift to the hospital, if you're headed that way? You mentioned Nick being there, and it would give me a chance to talk to him."

He wished he could say no and feel okay about it. But he couldn't. He'd spent the night and had had sex with her not once but twice. And if he now told her to find her own way to the hospital, it would make him seem like a jerk. At least in his own eyes.

"Sure." He'd planned on stopping home to shower and change, but he kept a spare set of clothes at the hospital for nights when he was on call. He could shower there, as well. No one would ever be the wiser. "Can you be ready in twenty?"

"Definitely." She closed the door. "Feel free to call down for room service if you want something to eat. They're pretty quick as long as you stick to the quick fare menu."

Room service. It figured.

"I can wait until I get to the hospital." He paused. "Do you want me to call down for something for you?"

"No, I'm not a big breakfast eater. I'll just grab some coffee at the hospital."

Thirty minutes later, they pulled up to the hospital and Luke parked his little car. As they walked through the entrance, a voice came from their left. "Kate?"

Luke glanced toward the sound.

Dammit. The very person he'd hoped to avoid this morning. Nick was walking down the hallway with Tiggy beside him.

Nick cocked his head, as if realizing for the first time that Luke was with her. "Hey, how lucky is this, to all run into each other at the same time?"

Luke held out his hand and shook Nick's. "Lucky indeed."

Unfortunately, out of the corner of his eye he noticed Kate's face go through a series of subtle color changes before it settled on pink. Bright pink.

She leaned up to give the other man a kiss on the cheek then smiled at Tiggy. "Luke was just telling me y'all might be here today."

He couldn't help but notice the typical southern expression, or Nick's smile, which signaled the other man had caught it as well.

"A few more minutes and you would have missed

us," Nick said, stretching his back. "Did you happen to ask Luke about next week?"

Next week? Now what had the woman gone and done?

"Oh, um. No. I thought you might like to do it yourself."

He reached a hand toward his wife, who took hold of it in both of hers. "We want you both to come and have dinner at our house next week."

Luke went very still. Kate knew about this and was supposed to tell him? And yet she'd said nothing?

She was unbelievable. First she wanted him to put in a good word for her at the rehab center, and now she was busy planning dinner engagements for him as if they were a frigging couple or something.

"And I take it Kate has already said yes."

"She has."

He sent her a sideways glare, noting her eyes were wide. With guilt? "She accepted for the both of us?"

"No, but I'm sure she'd be glad if you came."

"She would, would she?" Luke's eyes continued to zero in on her like laser scalpels, slicing his way to the truth.

As if realizing something was off between the two of them, Nick frowned, his glance skipping over him. Luke was well aware his clothes were wrinkled and he had a day's worth of stubble on his chin—things he'd hoped to remedy by the time he saw his friend.

"Are you just getting off work?" he said. "I thought you mentioned coming on duty about the time I finished with therapy."

Great. Now what?

Kate was no help. She was staring at the pattern in

the floor as if it had ancient Sanskrit writings hidden within it.

"No, I was out last night. Just getting in, in fact. I thought I'd shower here at the hospital."

Nick's attention turned to Kate, who, thank heavens, was much better groomed and who'd had a quick shower back at the hotel. "Well, I'm glad I caught you before I left."

Tiggy let go of his hand and dug around in her purse. "You already know where we live, but I wanted to give you our mobile numbers in case you need to get hold of us. We were thinking Tuesday evening. Could you come round at sixish? Would that work for both of you?"

Kate's head came up. "Fine with me."

It was too much to hope that he was on duty that night—but Luke didn't think he was. "I'll check my schedule and get back with you."

"I'm sure you'd love him to come, wouldn't you, Kate?"

Her eyes came up to meet his, and Luke swore he saw the barest hint of an apology in their blue depths. "Definitely. It wouldn't be the same without him."

CHAPTER TEN

THE REHAB CENTER was modern and up-to-date, and Kate had been totally shocked when Luke called her that afternoon and said he'd arranged a tour—if she still wanted to see it. She did.

Laisse, one of the physical therapists, smiled at her. "Dr. Blackman tells me you're well versed in LSVT therapy."

Warmth spread through her chest. He'd actually remembered the name of it? "I'm a licensed physical therapist, but I also have my LSVT certification."

"Which tract? Big or Loud?"

"Both, but I've dealt more with the Big side of the spectrum as it deals with body movements, rather than the speech element. My father has Parkinson's—early stage—so I thought I might be able to help him with therapy. Turns out he's got a great therapist and hasn't needed me."

"So what brings you to London?"

This is where it got tricky, and for the first time she wished Luke was here to smooth the way for her. "I have a relative who was a patient here." Hopefully that would be enough of an explanation.

"Oh, I hope everything went well."

"It did. He's finishing up his treatment and should be fine."

Laisse stopped in front of an older woman, who was using an upper-body ergometer. The machine looked much like a bulky, gray stationary bike that had been turned on its head, and gave a steady whine as the woman pedaled with her hands, warming up her muscles before getting down to whatever therapies she would need. "How are we doing, Mrs. Wheaton?"

"It's a bit harder than I expected." Her breath rasped in and out as she struggled to keep pumping.

Laisse bent over and looked at the dial, twisting it to reduce the resistance level. "How's that? Better? I don't want to wear you out before our session."

"Yes, much easier, thank you."

"Do you think you can manage another two minutes?"

The woman nodded, her hands circling a bit faster.

They continued their tour. "Our LSVT therapist isn't here today, I'm sorry to say. She's due in tomorrow, if you'd like to come back."

"Would it be possible for me to observe her with a patient?"

"I'll check with the head therapist, but I don't think it will be a problem. We have relatives in quite a bit, watching as their loved ones have therapy. I'm sure Steffie wouldn't mind."

They stopped by the front desk and Laisse scribbled a note on a pad on the counter. "What was your last name again?"

"Bradley."

"Okay, Kate. I've got you down." She ran a finger down a black scheduling book. "Steffie's first appointment is at nine tomorrow. Let me check with her before

I say yes, but I don't expect there to be a problem. Why don't you come in at ten, if that's all right? She has several patients in a row."

"Wonderful." Kate pulled out her wallet and found one of her business cards. She wrote the hotel's phone number and her room number on the back. "This is where I'm staying. If there's a problem, would you mind giving me a call?"

"Of course." The whine of the ergometer slowed and then came to a halt. Laisse glanced over at the machine. "I need to get back to my patient, but I'll see you tomorrow, then."

"Yes. Thanks again for the tour. You have a beautiful facility."

Laisse looked around with pride. "Thank you. We're quite proud of it."

Shoving her wallet back in her purse, Kate glanced at the glass wall to her right, her fingers fumbling a bit when she spied Luke outside, looking in at her. What did he want? She assumed that once he'd dropped her off at the center, he'd wash his hands of her. Their last joint appearance would be at Nick's house for dinner and after that they'd each go their own way.

"Okay, I'll see you tomorrow. Thanks again."

"My pleasure." Laisse's voice lowered to almost a purr as she, too, noted who was on the other side of the viewing glass.

Kate squashed the urge to roll her eyes. "Do you know Dr. Blackman?"

"Not well. He introduced himself when he made your appointment. But I've heard quite a bit about him."

What did she mean? "Really?"

"He has quite a reputation with the nurses on the wards."

The image of all those letters in her mom's shoebox came back to haunt her, and she bit her lip. Luke certainly knew his way around a bedroom. A flush came over her as she remembered exactly the way he'd taken charge.

At the time she'd thought it was sensual beyond belief, but what if he was just like a male version of her mother? Someone who jumped from person to person, leaving behind a trail of broken hearts? She'd been worried about her own genetic traits after she'd leaped into bed with him, but maybe she wasn't the person she should be worried about.

Laisse turned away from the window with obvious reluctance and headed for her patient.

That settled it, then. Reputations didn't materialize out of thin air. And the other physical therapist certainly didn't seem opposed to having Luke come into the center. But no way did she want to watch Laisse fawn over him.

And Kate definitely didn't want to wind up as a letter in someone's shoebox. It was time to steer clear of him actively. It wouldn't be hard to do because she didn't work at the hospital and would be going home before too much longer.

She glanced at the window again, only to see him nod at her, his hands shoved into the pockets of his slacks. His white lab coat was nowhere to be seen. Great. Hopefully that didn't mean he was off duty.

Well, she was going to have to walk through that door some time, especially as Laisse was already working with her patient, although she'd seen the other woman peer in Luke's direction another time or two.

Making her way across the room, she reached the

glass door and pushed through it. Luke met her on the other side. "How did it go?" he asked.

"Pretty well. I'm going to come by and observe the LSVT therapist tomorrow morning."

"Good." He took her elbow and started to steer her away from the area. She frowned until she noted that Laisse was watching them.

Why did she get the feeling she was about to be added to the gossip swirling around Luke? She tugged her elbow out of his hold. "Did you need to see me about something?"

"I wanted to let you know that I'll be able to go to Nick's."

What did he expect her to say? That she was thrilled? Ecstatic? Horrified? She settled for none of the above. "Nick will be happy to hear that."

"I figured." He paused. "Listen, about what happened at your hotel room, I'd really prefer Nick not know."

She blinked in surprise and then let out a little laugh. "Oh, how the worm has turned. Wasn't it me who was worried about that very thing just a few days ago? I remember some doctor letting me stew in my own juices for a few moments before promising he wouldn't say anything."

Luke hooked his index finger under her chin, his thumb making a long slow pass over her lower lip. "So, are you going to make me stew in my own juices to get your revenge?"

No, because he'd probably have the last laugh. Somehow.

"Of course not. I'm not about to say anything to anyone. It's not something *I'm* likely to brag about."

His eyes narrowed just a bit. "Meaning?"

She glanced back at the viewing window, but Laisse was busy with her patient. At least, she appeared to be. "It's just that people around here appear to be inordinately interested in your…nocturnal activities."

His face cleared. "Ah, I see." His thumb still rested on her lower lip, and this time, instead of sliding across it, he tugged the center of it down, parting her lips for a heart-stopping second. Then he released her with a smile. "Nick seemed to be worried I might try to take advantage of you."

So even Nick had the idea that Luke slept around.

Wow. And now she'd been with him twice. No… three times, if you counted the two-in-one-night episode in her hotel room. Insisting on giving him that massage had been the dumbest idea she'd ever had.

"Well, good thing he was wrong. Isn't it? About you taking advantage of me, I mean."

"Definitely. Besides, I seem to remember it being the other way around."

Her eyes widened. Surely he didn't think…

"I didn't take advantage of anyone."

His smile widened. "No?" He moved in, lowering his head as if to keep their conversation private. "Let's see. I asked you to meet me down in the parking lot with my car keys. Instead, you invited me up to your hotel room. Hmm…actually *invited* is kind of a mild word. It might be closer to the truth to say you forced me to come up."

"I didn't force you to do anything." But she had, and she knew it. She'd said she lost the keys and then, when he'd come to her room to get them, she'd manipulated him into a massage.

But *Luke* was the one who'd initiated that devastating kiss.

And she'd responded like there was no tomorrow.

He was right. Looking at it from his perspective, the evidence did seem pretty damning.

"I was honestly trying to help, Luke. Things just kind of got out of hand."

"Hey, I was kidding. It was as much my fault as anyone's." He gave her hand a quick squeeze. "And all that talk around here? Don't believe everything you hear."

"So you haven't slept with anyone from the hospital?"

Why on earth had she asked that? It was none of her business who he did or didn't sleep with.

He hesitated, his smile fading. "Would you like me to give you names and dates?"

"No. I really wouldn't." She sucked in a quick breath, a shard of hurt burrowing deep. "Well, thanks for letting me know about dinner at Nick's. I'll let you get back to work."

"I'll walk you out."

"Oh, no need." All she wanted to do at the moment was get as far away from him as she could.

"At the risk of sounding like a broken record, you never did get that personal item out of my glove compartment."

Oh, heavens. With the chaos at the accident scene and having to drive his car back to the hotel afterward, she'd completely forgotten. Which meant her opportunity for a painless transition of bag to purse was long gone. Unlike her, he'd evidently remembered what was in there and had checked to see if she'd taken it with her. Time to put this little piece of history to bed.

She almost groaned aloud at that thought. "Let's get this over with."

He slanted her a glance that she couldn't read then

headed for the exit down the hallway. Kate followed him, the physical therapist within her taking over and looking for signs that his leg bothered him.

Right leg. Left leg. *Blip*. Right leg.

Yep, there it was. If you didn't know he had a problem, you'd miss it completely. The tiniest limp when his left leg lifted off the ground, transferring his full weight onto his right. He covered it well, but there was almost a forced look to his gait as if he'd learned to compensate. To make things appear normal when they really weren't.

Not wanting to show weakness.

Before they could make it to the door, a nurse came skidding around the corner and hurried toward them, her shoes squeaking on the polished flooring. "Dr. Blackman! Thank heavens I caught you before you left. Mindy Reynolds is asking to speak with you about her daughter. She's quite insistent."

Luke nodded and glanced at Kate. "She's a *patient*," he emphasized in low tones, as if remembering her question a few seconds ago.

"Oh, I never thought…" She swallowed the words, aware the nurse was still waiting there expectantly.

"I'll be there in just a minute." As the nurse walked away, he sighed. "Sorry, I have to go. I'll have to give you back that item we spoke of another time."

"Don't worry about them. Really." It was on the tip of her tongue to say she had plenty where that had come from, but it didn't seem appropriate.

"I'm not worried, Kate. I just don't believe in keeping things that don't belong to me."

As he turned and strolled in the direction the nurse had gone, his gait careful and even, she couldn't help but think he was giving her a subtle warning with that last line. He didn't keep things that didn't belong to him...including her.

CHAPTER ELEVEN

KATE TIGHTENED HER ponytail holder, slinging the towel around her neck as she switched off the treadmill in the hotel's exercise area, doing some quick calculations to convert kilometers into miles. The guy on the machine next to hers continued to jabber about his work problems—and his all-too-personal problems—seemingly oblivious that she was anxious to leave, despite only getting in two of her normal three miles.

Nothing was more charming than a man using his broken marriage to garner sympathy from other women—and hopefully getting laid in the process.

Kate wasn't buying a word of it. And she was more than anxious to make her getaway. "Well, have a good run."

To her irritation, he switched his machine off, as well. "I was just finishing." He shoved his surfer-blond hair out of his eyes with a muscular forearm. "Would you like to get a drink a little later in the bar?"

"I don't think your wife would exactly approve of that." She injected just enough irritation into her tone to show she wasn't interested in drinks, or anything else.

He swabbed down his face with the hotel towel. "Don't be like that. It's just a drink."

"I don't think so. I already have other plans." Like hell she did, but he didn't need to know that.

Kate headed for the door, the man hot on her heels—still trying to sweet-talk her. If this guy didn't buzz off pretty soon, those neglected body parts he'd mentioned were going to get some intimate attention—from the sharp edge of her knee.

He might be strong and reasonably attractive, but he made her feel nothing but revulsion. In a way it was a good sign. She really wouldn't leap into bed with any pretty face.

Just as she rounded the corner to the lobby she spied a familiar form speaking to the receptionist at the front desk.

Luke!

She had no idea what he was doing there, but she had never been so glad to see anyone in her life. He'd just slid a manila envelope across the counter top and turned to leave when his eyes found hers. She gave a wide, delighted smile. "Hey, there, stranger!"

The guy behind her stopped as well, settling in next to her.

Luke's brows lifted at her enthusiastic greeting then took in her workout gear, sliding up to her face before shifting to the jerk next to her. "Hi, yourself." He inclined his head toward the desk. "I was just dropping off your…belongings."

A peeved voice next to her said, "So your plans include this guy?"

She didn't turn her head to look but gave Luke a pleading glance. "As a matter of fact, they do. So, if you'll excuse me…"

Thankfully, Luke took the hint and made his way over to her. He gripped the ends of the towel around her neck and used them to draw her close, dropping a soft, lingering kiss on her lips that left her reeling. "Is this a workout buddy?" he murmured, keeping hold of the towel and giving the guy a level look.

Whatever silent communication passed between the two men seemed to work, because the weirdo edged a few steps to the side, putting some distance between them.

"Actually, I was just leaving." He nodded toward Kate. "Maybe I'll catch you in the exercise room tomorrow."

"I don't think so. I normally run at night." Which meant that if he tried to join her at night, she'd be free to run in the mornings again. Feeling strangely brave now that Luke was beside her, she glanced at the guy's zipper area. "Good luck with that little problem of yours."

The man's face flushed bright red and anger sizzled in his eyes before he glanced at Luke again. "Right. See you."

As soon as he'd stepped into the elevator, Kate sagged. "Sorry to put you in the middle of that. He wouldn't take no for an answer."

"Can't say I blame him." He let go of the towel. "Why didn't you just leave?"

"I did. I quit at two miles instead of three."

"You run three miles a day?"

Something in his voice made her look up at him. "Not every day, but most. Why?"

"No reason." He glanced in the direction of the elevators. "Do you normally wind up with a crew of men following you?"

Wondering if he thought she was being careless about safety, she said, "I used to run with my dad, until his Parkinson's diagnosis." She shrugged. "I haven't found another running partner yet but I don't purposely try to pick up guys. And since I was using the hotel's exercise room, I figured it was safe."

His fingers went to his leg, in an unconscious gesture that Kate found heart-wrenching.

She nodded at it. "How's it doing?"

"Fine." He drew in a determined breath. "Well, like I said, I left an envelope for you at the desk. The one from the glove compartment. Figured we needed to settle that account once and for all."

I don't believe in keeping things that don't belong to me.

And if someone *wanted* to belong to him?

What? She didn't! Not at all.

"Oh, okay. Well, thank you."

"I went ahead and washed them." His eyes held hers for several seconds as her face slowly ignited at the thought of her panties in with the rest of his clothes—mingling and touching parts of him. The slightest smile tipped the corners of his mouth as if he knew exactly what she was thinking. "I'll see you Tuesday evening, then."

At Nick's.

"I guess you will."

He hesitated, glancing at the elevators as if expecting the other guy to rematerialize at any second. "Would you like a ride? The hotel is right on my way."

Why did that offer make her heart sit up and blink? "That would be great, if you're sure."

"I am." He touched her cheek and then took a couple of steps back. "Be careful, Kate."

Be careful of the creepy workout buddy, not of him, right?

Then why did she feel like the warning was directed

at something much more personal than hotel exercise rooms?

And why did she feel the urge to take that warning and toss it to the wind?

CHAPTER TWELVE

THE FRONT DOOR opened and Nick stood there in a pair of black track pants and a matching T-shirt. "Sorry for the casual attire, but comfortable clothing is easier on my back right now."

Luke shook hands with him and stepped aside to reveal Kate, who was standing behind him. "Kate's hotel is on the way here, so I picked her up."

"Thoughtful of you." Nick's eyes narrowed just a touch as he looked from one to the other. "Hello, Kate."

"Hi." She came around and kissed his cheek. "Thank you again for inviting me over."

A voice came from inside the house. "Don't leave them out on the porch, love. Invite them in."

He smiled and lifted his brows. "I'm just doing that now." He stood aside and gestured them inside. "Tiggy's just putting the finishing touches to the salad."

"I'll go see if I can help her."

Kate called out to the other woman, and Tiggy answered, leaving Luke alone in the entryway with Nick. The man's eyes were shrewder than he remembered.

"So how's it going with Kate?"

"Going?"

"With making me look good."

Luke's muscles relaxed. "I think she's basically there.

Not much more I can do, she just needs to get to know you over a period of time. How's Tiggy handling everything?"

"Surprisingly well." The other man led the way into a small, darkly paneled sitting area. "Would you like something to drink?"

"Whiskey, if you have it."

Nick took down two cut-glass tumblers from inside a cabinet and poured them each a drink. "Have a seat."

Why did he get the feeling he was about to be interrogated? Not that he blamed his friend, but he could ask Luke about Kate until he was blue in the face. He'd promised her he wouldn't say anything, and she'd promised to return the favor. He wouldn't be the one to crack under the pressure.

Besides, seeing her in that workout gear yesterday had driven home the differences between them. She was young and strong, able to do whatever she wanted physically. And when she'd talked about finding a running buddy, he'd realized he'd never be able to be that. For anyone.

Nick handed him the glass then sat in a chair across from his. "How did your dinner date go?"

How the hell did he know about that? He glanced at the door wondering if maybe Kate had—

"Relax. I'm not accusing you of doing anything. You'd mentioned taking her out to talk about my diagnosis. How is she dealing with finding out about me?" He took a sip of his drink. "I can see what's on the surface, but not what's going on underneath."

"I don't think she knows what to think. She doesn't have anything against you personally, it's just been a shock, from what I can gather." Luke took a healthy swallow of his drink. He'd have to be careful as he was driving Kate home tonight. And that was all he'd be doing.

His lecture to himself did as much good this time as it had last time. While his head knew he wasn't the right person for her, his body was in strong disagreement. It was telling him they were compatible in every way that mattered.

Well, buddy, as hard as it is for you to comprehend, that's not all there is to life.

"It's been a shock for all of us," Nick said.

"I can imagine. She did ask if she could see the physical therapy area at the hospital. So I took her over there."

"Was she looking for me? I was there on Saturday, but I think they've done about all they can for me." Nick sat with his back well away from the chair cushion, he noticed.

"How did things go?"

"It's been a damned hard road. But I'm determined to get back to where I was—for the baby's sake."

If only hard work was all it took to get there. Luke had worked his ass off and he was still nowhere near where he had once been. And he never would be. He'd never be able to chase a soccer ball across a field with his son. Never be able to swing his daughter round and round and listen to her squeal with happiness.

He shook away the thoughts. He'd accepted all of that years ago, so why was he suddenly torturing himself again?

He could still do his job, and that was all that mattered. He should be happy. Fulfilled. And he knew there were others who were a whole lot worse off than he was. So it was time to stop moping over stupid inconsequential things.

Such as not being able to run like other men.

As if some switch in his brain had been tripped into the "on" position, a vision of the muscle-bound hulk next to Kate came to life in his head, reviving yearnings he'd thought long dead. Stupid, unattainable desires of physical capability.

"Luke, are you all right?"

"What? I'm sorry, did you say something?" It was then that he realized it wasn't just Nick staring at him. Tiggy and Kate were now in the room as well—Tiggy propped on the arm of Nick's chair and Kate on the brown leather sofa across from them. All eyes were fastened firmly on him. Kate had a worried frown on her face as she stared at his groin area.

No, not his groin. Lower.

It was then he felt the pain of his fingers digging into the muscles of his right leg. Torturing it for failing him at every turn.

He released his hold, laying his palm flat on the fabric of his jeans. "Yeah, I'm fine. Sorry, had my mind on a case."

Kate's brows lifted a centimeter in question. She knew he was lying.

Don't ask it. Not in front of them.

Nick saved the day by turning to her instead. "I hear you were checking out the rehabilitation facilities over at the hospital."

"Yes, I wanted to see what they offered." She proceeded to talk about her LSVT training, answering questions as Tiggy or Nick voiced them, her face alive and animated, hands gesturing as she described different techniques. She loved her job as much as Luke loved his.

When the conversation inevitably rolled around to

her adoptive father back in Memphis, Kate grew hesitant, obviously not wanting to offend Nick or Tiggy. "He's been great about everything."

"How long are you planning on staying in London?" Nick draped his arm around Tiggy's waist. "We'd love to have you around for a while."

"I don't know." Again there was that strange hesitation. "Like I said, my dad has Parkinson's. I want to be available to help him however I can."

It had to be incredibly awkward for her to use the words *dad* and *father* when referring to the man who'd raised her. But then again, what else would she call him?

"Will you go back to your old job?"

"Possibly. They're holding it open for me, just in case. But they know my plans are kind of fluid right now."

So she wasn't just taking vacation time. He again wondered whether Kate was thinking about making a change, despite her father's Parkinson's diagnosis. If so, it would be a pretty drastic one.

Hadn't he done the same thing when he'd moved from Chicago to London? The difference was that Luke had nothing to hold him in the States. His mom and dad were divorced, and aside from the money he sent to his mother on a regular basis, she'd never shown any interest in having him come for a visit. And his dad... It would be better if Luke never saw him again.

Tiggy stood. "Well, I think everything is ready."

She hovered over her husband for a moment, as if making sure he was okay, before he shooed her away. "I'm fine."

They sat down at the dining room table and passed around roast beef and potatoes. Luke stretched his injured leg under the table, bumping Kate's foot by accident.

Her gaze jerked up, eyes widening, but she didn't move or say anything. Neither did he. In fact, he kept his foot right where it was—touching hers—in a game of chicken.

Who would move away first?

Everyone continued talking as if nothing was amiss, but that small area of contact burned through Luke, slowly traveling up his leg until it reached dangerous heights.

Kate blinked and stabbed a piece of meat with her fork, bringing it up to her mouth. On impulse, he slid his foot a little farther forward and hooked it around hers. She stopped chewing for a second or two.

He was playing a dangerous game, and he knew it. He'd basically promised Nick to refrain from any hanky-panky, and here he was playing footsie with the man's daughter under his own table. But there was something reckless and dangerous about it, and he couldn't seem to make himself draw back.

Neither did she pull free, which just heightened the temptation to push things a little further, toying with forbidden fruit right under her father's nose.

What the hell was wrong with him? He wasn't a hormonal sixteen-year-old boy anymore, but here he was, behaving like one.

All he could think of was that while Kate had shunned that muscle-bound clod's advances, she was definitely not using her eyes to plead with Nick to rescue her like she had with him.

And that just sent another wave of heat spiking through him, making him want to up the ante. Just how far would she let him go?

He used the back of her foot to tip off his loafer, which he dragged back to his chair. The tablecloth was long enough that no one could see a thing. He then edged back toward her, using his socked toes to tug at the back of her left high heel. She grabbed her water glass and took a long sip as he casually answered something Nick had asked. When he turned his attention back to Kate, she surprised him by lifting her foot and allowing him to prise off her shoe.

Her look said, *Are you crazy*?

Probably. He had no idea why he was doing this. Was it the risk of discovery, like in the supply closet?

No, that encounter had had nothing to do with the taboo of public sex and everything to do with sheer need. He'd wanted her. And she'd apparently wanted him just as much.

He eased her shoe to the side and slid his foot up and over hers, while Kate carefully set down her water glass and wrapped her hands around her fork and knife. Probably wondering where to stab him first.

But, damn the woman, she wasn't scrabbling around for her shoe or trying to shove her foot back into it. Or trying to brush him off like she had The Persistent Hulk.

Luke wanted to see how far he could push her. Well, he might end up being the first to back down from this little encounter. Hmm. Time to send her running for the hills.

He gave her a slow smile. "So how does one decide to spend a lifetime trying various massage techniques on helpless patients?"

He was gratified to see color wash up her neck and settle in her cheeks. Not so gratified to see the scowl cross Nick's face.

A little too obvious?

Maybe. But he was feeling just a little bit desperate.

His toes edged up past the hem of her beige slacks, remembering exactly how the back pockets had hugged her delectable bottom. Her tongue moistened her lips as he ventured a bit higher.

"I wouldn't exactly call them helpless." She let go of her silverware and crossed her forearms on the edge of the table, leaning forward a bit. "Some of them are strong enough to heft, say, a hundred and twenty pounds, without batting an eyelid."

"Interesting number, that." He eyed her, his smile growing. She was skating on ice that was just as thin as his was.

Nick and Tiggy seemed oblivious to the suggestive comments winging back and forth across the table, but he was eventually going to have to call a halt to this particular game before things went too far.

"How about dessert?" Tiggy said, standing to clear plates.

When Kate started to join her, the other woman waved her away. "Stay there and enjoy yourself. I'll just be a minute."

"Thank you." Her leg suddenly pulled out of reach, and just as Luke thought he might emerge the victor, a weight settled on his good knee. Hell, she'd just propped her heel on him.

His smile widened. All the better.

Luke asked Nick about his work, making sure the question required a long-drawn-out answer, and then slipped his hand beneath the tablecloth, capturing Kate's foot before she had a chance to realize what he was doing and make her escape.

He heard her quick intake of breath as his fingers cupped her instep, his thumb massaging the curve of her arch. She squirmed and tried to pull away, but he held her fast. He couldn't tell if the sensation was just ticklish or if it was as heady to her as it was to him. Touching her skin to skin was suddenly bringing back a whole lot of memories. And bringing a lot of things to life that should be left napping.

Along with that came a terrible realization. He needed to have her again.

Kate's eyes were on Nick as he spoke, but her teeth came down on her lip as if trying to contain the sounds that might be bubbling up in her throat. And he wanted to hear them again. Each and every one.

Tiggy came back with a tray of coffee and pastries and served them each a generous portion.

If Kate thought she was finally going to be able to pull free, she was very much mistaken. He could cut and eat his dessert with just one hand without any problem. Because his other hand was occupied at the moment.

"So, do you have any plans over the next couple of days?" Tiggy asked Kate.

Luke spoke up. "I was planning on showing Kate some sights later on."

"How nice." Nick smiled, probably thinking Luke was looking for another opportunity to extol his virtues. "Big Ben is lovely at night."

"Yes, there is that. There are a few other things I'd like her to see, as well."

Kate shifted a bit, as if catching his drift. "I'm looking forward to it."

Little did Nick and Tiggy know they'd helped aid and abet the very thing Nick was worried about. Luke had just propositioned Kate right under their noses, and she'd accepted without batting an eyelid.

CHAPTER THIRTEEN

THE SECOND THEY were back in Luke's car in the parking garage, his lips were on hers. As if the dam holding back all her pent-up desires had suddenly burst under the pressure, she moaned loudly, glad to finally let the sound out. Both hands went to the back of his neck, holding him close. The tiny hairs at his nape tickled, bringing home the reality that he really was here—kissing her like he couldn't get enough. She wanted to be closer. Wanted him right now.

"What the hell were you playing at back there?" The low words muttered against her mouth made her see stars.

She bit his lip then sucked it into her mouth, her breath coming in shallow gusts. "I didn't start that particular game. But I was certainly willing to finish it."

He swore softly. "So you're saying if I'd thrown you on top of that dining room table in front of Nick and Tiggy…"

"I'm saying I wouldn't have stopped you."

He moved in for another breath-stealing kiss. "Hell, woman, you're impossible. No wonder that guy back at the hotel didn't want to give up."

"He didn't have a chance."

His fingers tunneled in her hair. "And I do?"

"What do you think?"

"I think if this garage didn't have a whole slew of cameras…"

He'd actually thought of taking her right here? Oh, man. Damn those cameras, anyway!

"There's always my hotel room." She'd think about the repercussions later.

"No. I think I want you in *my* bed this time. Where I can do as I please."

Kate shivered in reaction. How on earth did he make everything sound like a sensual promise?

Because he himself was temptation incarnate.

"This time you're doing all the work, then." Not that she wanted him to. She just couldn't think of a single witty thing to say that was as bold as he was.

"Oh, Kate, I wouldn't have it any other way. You won't have to lift a finger. I promise."

She couldn't lift a finger.

Literally.

Luke had gone from holding her wrists over her head on the bed as he kissed her to pressing a finger to her lips and walking to his closet, coming back with a brown leather belt wrapped around his hand.

Uh, if he was into whipping or something, she was out of there.

"Wha—?"

"Shh. I'm not going to hurt you. It's my turn to do all the work, remember?"

He placed her hands on either side of a metal rung on the bed's headboard and then wrapped the flexible leather around her hands and the post, sliding the loop through the buckle, tightening it enough to hold her there, but not enough to cut off her circulation. He then repeated the act a couple of times until she had several layers around her wrists in a way that wouldn't come undone on their own. Her hands were now trapped.

She'd never been tied up before, and wasn't sure she'd like it, but his lips were on her cheek as he spoke softly to her. That, along with the feeling of helplessness, added another layer of sensuality. Luke had already proved he wouldn't hurt her. She was pretty sure if she started panicking, he'd release her immediately.

She didn't want to be released. Not yet. Maybe not ever.

Luke got off the bed and the lights clicked off, throwing the room into complete darkness. Kate frowned. She wanted to see him this time. "Luke, can't we—?"

"No. My turn to do all the work, remember? That means I make the decisions."

Great. She'd made that stupid comment and now she was going to have to suffer the consequences. Although *suffering* wasn't exactly the word she would use.

Warm lips touched her cheek again and slid over to her ear in a soft caress. "Unless you'd rather I blindfold you instead."

"I wouldn't be able to see you, either way." she groused.

"No, Kate, you wouldn't." His breath was warm, and she shivered again. "But I'd be able to see you."

She'd be lying there naked and exposed for his viewing pleasure while she was kept in utter darkness.

"Not fair." She forced a laugh, but it came out strangled.

"I never said I was going to play fair." The bed gave as he sat next to her. "So which will it be? Lights or blindfold?"

"Lights."

"Now, that's just a damn shame." He stroked her jaw, letting his hand trail down the line of her throat. When he reached the top button of her blouse, he flicked it open with nimble fingers. He moved on to the next one. "I like this shirt. I can unbutton it and spread it open…like this."

The front edges of her shirt were peeled apart and laid on the bed.

His hands glided across her abdomen, just his fingertips touching her. Goose bumps broke out over her flesh as he made his way up to her bra. He tapped the plastic fastener in the hollow of her breasts.

"I like this, as well."

He unclipped it and drew the edges sideways, forcing the fabric to slide slowly over her nipples as it went. They reacted instantly, and she pushed them upward almost against her will, the contact over far too quickly.

And Luke didn't seem in a hurry to replace the bra with his hands—or, better yet, his mouth.

Still sitting, he touched her imprisoned wrists, easing his fingers down the sensitive skin on the insides of her forearms, gliding past her elbows until he reached her shoulders.

He turned his hands over, his knuckles skimming the sides of her breasts, barely avoiding the nipple area, which was screaming for his touch. He repeated the gesture.

He wasn't into whipping. He was into torture instead.

On the third pass, with no relief in sight, she groaned. "Luke, please."

Sliding his hands under the back of her rib cage, his thumbs continued to stroke the sides of her breasts. Circling without touching the end zone. "What do you want, Kate?"

She swallowed. Was he going to make her say it?

"Tell me." His thumbs swept up the sides again, almost, almost grazing the right spot.

"I want you to touch me." The whispered words came out of their own accord.

His fingers paused in midstroke, just beyond reach. "Where?"

God, she wanted her hands free so she could show him instead.

She sucked down a couple of deep breaths, her body seething with need as she tried to screw up the courage. "M-my nipples."

"Your nipples. Mmm. Like this?" His thumbs gave a single sweet stroke across the sensitive buds and pure sensation streaked from her breasts straight down to her groin. A raw, tremulous sound erupted from her throat, and she strained against the leather belt holding her in place.

He didn't make her beg again but centered his attention right where she'd asked, murmuring his approval when she arched into his hands to increase the contact. He squeezed, his thumb and forefinger creating the most delicious mixture of pressure and friction imaginable, then leaned down and kissed her. Kate found herself trying to devour his mouth, her tongue seeking and finding his, rubbing against it like a needy cat. All the while he kept the main part of his attention centered on her breasts.

She wanted him inside her now. Needed him so badly. Dragging her mouth away, she squirmed and shifted, all the while trying to find the words inside her that would get her what she craved. "Luke, now. Please."

He immediately slowed, drawing his fingertips down

her stomach in long, soothing trails. "Not yet. Not for a while."

What? Surely he wasn't going to leave her hanging? Or, worse, leave her alone completely. They could go slow later. Or he could go as slow as he wanted to, she just needed…needed…

Release.

She squeezed her thighs together, her hips unconsciously rising and falling, seeking the kind of pressure she needed to get over the top of that mountain.

A knee wedged between hers. Thinking he was going to give her what she wanted, she quickly parted them wide for him. He moved onto the bed, kneeling between her legs before going down on his haunches, making no move to remove his clothing. Or to lie on top of her. All he did was continue to stroke her sensitized skin, avoiding all the important areas.

"Luke, what are you doing?"

She saw the glint of his teeth in the darkness. "I said not yet."

Too late, she realized he'd tricked her into separating her thighs, preventing her from using them to bring herself to completion. "No!"

"Yes." He leaned over and nipped her jaw. "You'll thank me later. I promise."

No, she wouldn't. Only someone with a sadistic sense of humor would say something like that.

Then his lips went to her nipple and pulled hard. The sudden wet heat chased away all thoughts of revenge, replacing them with a clawing need that took right up where it had left off. He leaned up and grabbed the fabric of his polo shirt, yanking it over his head.

Finally!

Kate found her eyes had grown accustomed to the

gloom, and she could barely make out the shadow of his tattoo and the diagonal trail of the old knife wound on his chest. But she still couldn't see clearly enough to satisfy her.

Her hands flexed on the bedpost, wanting to run her fingers down his chest and unsnap the button to his khakis. But she couldn't. He'd seen to that.

He did slide backward, however, and undo hers. Unlike the last time, he didn't leave her panties on. Instead, he peeled both garments down her legs, until they were gone.

Then his mouth was on her inner knee, licking his way slowly up. She swallowed, the urge to snap her legs together thwarted by the fact that he was still between them. Why did she get the feeling that had been his plan all along?

Oh, he was devious. Merciless. And she might just thank him later after all.

If only he'd hurry it up!

He bit her inner thigh, unexpectedly, causing her to jump and moving her thoughts firmly back to him.

His hands went to her hips, fingers curling around them, holding her in place as he made his way higher, inch by inch. He might be trying to keep her from squirming, but that was impossible at this point. Her body was following each and every movement his lips made and trying to anticipate where they might head next…to maximize the contact.

His palms went under her butt and lifted, as if serving her up for his pleasure. And his first bite made her cry out.

"I love hearing you whimper when I touch you." He took a slow swipe with his tongue, eliciting a pained moan this time, while he watched her. "It makes me so fucking hard."

Her, too. Her parts might be different but, God, he hit her right where it counted.

He continued to stare over the planes and hills of her body, his eyes boring into hers. He slid his hands out from beneath her, her butt dropping back to the surface of the bed, while he stayed exactly where he was.

What? That was it?

He gave her a slow smile. "Do you want me, Kate?"

"You know I do." Her heart was thundering in her chest, begging him to finish her off. All it would take was a few more seconds.

"Show me."

How? Her hands were tied. She couldn't touch him. Could barely move anything except her pelvis.

He nodded. "Do it. Show me what you want."

As if her body were on a different astral plane from that of her conscious self, she planted the soles of her feet flat on the bed, bent her knees and slowly pushed herself up to his waiting mouth. Held herself there as he tasted her, nibbled…the whisper of hot air touching her sensitive flesh. All the while his eyes remained just above the horizon, focused on her, watching each and every reaction. That's why he wanted her pelvis up. So he could see her slowly unravel. He was a terrible, sexy voyeur who had absolutely no shame. Absolutely no…

His lips zeroed in on the tiny erect nub of flesh and surrounded it, tongue gliding across it in a long exquisite stroke that seemed to go on forever while she pressed harder and harder against him, her insides winding impossibly tight. From a distance she heard herself panting his name, her voice sliding up an imaginary scale of notes, until her eyelids screwed down tight. And she screamed. Long and loud, the release of doing so incredible. All the while his mouth held her prisoner, his hands returning to support her butt when she would have collapsed. He kept her there for several seconds until every muscle in her body released at once, going totally boneless.

Still he kissed her, until he'd coaxed every last twitch from her body.

"God," she whispered. "Oh, God." She thought she might have kept saying those words over and over, but she wasn't sure. Then he was there, finally on top of her, finally sliding into her body, filling her.

Kissing her lips. Smoothing her hair away from her damp brow.

She'd never be the same again. Ever. She still couldn't bring herself to move, even when he withdrew and pushed forward again. Then words came from shaking lips. "Thank you."

She'd said it. And she didn't care.

He reached up and undid the belt, freeing her hands, still deep inside her. As she shut her eyes and pulled in a deep sigh, he cupped her face and kissed her again. "That was just the beginning."

For him, maybe. She was shot. But she was perfectly willing to entertain him after the orgasm he'd just given her.

As if he was a mind reader, he muttered, "Do you think you're done, Kate? Do you think your body is done?" He edged deeper and touched a spot inside that flickered back to life, despite herself. "It's not. It just doesn't know it yet."

CHAPTER FOURTEEN

LUKE WAS DRESSED before she woke up. Just like he always was when he spent the night with someone.

It wasn't vanity. At least, he didn't think it was.

The fact that he didn't have a single full-length mirror in his house didn't mean a thing. He'd be the first to admit he couldn't stomach the sight of that atrophying, twisted lump of flesh he called a leg. The actual scars didn't faze him—he saw much worse on a daily basis at the hospital. It was what those scars represented that kept him from switching the lights on and making love like a normal person.

The sizzling scent of bacon brought his attention back to the skillet, and he adjusted the flame, turning the strips so they'd cook on the other side. The least he could do was feed her.

A slight smile tilted his lips as he remembered Kate's slim body writhing beneath his hands—pushing up toward his mouth. Yes, it was heady knowing he had the power to make her reach for her pleasure—to exercise a small amount of control over her. There was no denying it. But there was also method to his madness. He'd found the faster he got a woman to that plateau high above the easy petting and foreplay that went on in most relationships, the less likely she was to glance back toward earth and see him. The real him.

Then he could relax and enjoy her—enjoy the sex—without the elaborate maneuverings necessary to keep her attention off him. Once she was in the clouds, all he had to do was use his voice. Direct her. Keep her focused on her own body.

And the shorter the relationship was afterward, the less likely a woman was to want to cuddle on the couch. To start probing a little too deeply. Or insist the lights stay on.

Like Kate had tried to do.

He glanced down at his pants leg. No one would ever guess what was just below that fabric...and what lay deep beneath the skin, muscle and bone. Luke had become that leg. Obsessed with what its weakness had cost him.

Damn it!

Why was he slogging through all this again?

Because he knew his time with Kate needed to come to an end. Soon. Not just because of Nick—although not keeping his word on that front was eating at him—but also because that's the way it had to be. The way it had always been.

"Hey, why didn't you wake me up?"

Kate stood in the doorway, draped in one of his white dress shirts. She didn't have it buttoned up the front, just wrapped around her waist like a bathrobe. Her folded arms held it in place. Little did she know that doing so pulled the fabric taut against her breasts, the rosy outlines of her nipples clearly visible. Or maybe she did know.

Glancing at her face, he saw nothing but a puzzled question. She didn't understand why he hadn't woken her up, it was as simple as that. Nothing coy or cunning about her.

Unlike him, who'd manipulated her exactly where he'd wanted her.

He swallowed. Yep, he was as ugly inside as that damned leg. Maybe uglier.

"I thought you might like to sleep."

"Do you have to work?"

"Yes, in about an hour."

She pulled the shirt tighter. "Were you going to wake me at all?"

Of course he was. But not until the last minute, when she'd be forced to eat quickly so he could drive her back to the hotel.

Picking up a plate, he laid the bacon onto the paper towels covering it, choosing his words carefully. "I was going to let you sleep as long as possible, but, yes, I was going to wake you up."

She took a couple of steps closer, and he held the plate out, offering her some of the meat. She shook her head. "I need to go shower and get dressed."

"Your clothes are folded in the bathroom."

"Let me guess. You washed them."

There was an acid tinge to her voice that made him look at her a little closer. Should he not have washed them?

"Is something wrong?"

She shut her eyes and pulled in a deep breath. "No. Sorry. I just didn't mean to wind up here."

"At my house?"

"Among other things."

He set the plate down and moved toward her. "You seemed to enjoy it well enough."

She laughed. "Oh, I did. That's not the problem."

Strange. He was the one who normally went down this particular road. According to his mental GPS, it was called Regret Avenue, and he seemed to wind up there a lot.

"Hey, it's okay." He combed his fingers through her soft hair and let it fan out around her shoulders. "We're both consenting adults. We had a little fun. No one was injured. At least, I don't think anyone was." His thumb skimmed over her jaw. "I didn't hurt you, did I?"

"No, of course not. It's just that my mom…" She shook her head. "Never mind. You're right. It was fun. And now it's…"

She didn't finish the thought, but he could fill in the blank. *And now it's over.*

So why was he chafing at the thought? Because she was fun and honest and sexy, a combination he found lethal.

"Why don't you go get your shower and I'll make some toast and eggs to go along with this? How do you like yours?"

"I like them unbroken."

"Excuse me?" There was a wistfulness in her voice that made him squirm inside.

"Sorry. The eggs. I like them hard boiled."

Why did he think she was talking about something other than the eggs?

She was only in London for a little while, as was he. And even if they *had* been from the same geographical location in the States, it wasn't likely they could take things to the next level, even if he wanted to. Which he didn't. This was a vacation fling on her part, and a very pleasant encounter on his.

Nick came back to mind. His friend had slept with a tourist and had ended up fathering a child. Was she thinking that both her biological father and the man whose life he'd saved were both shallow bastards, happy with a quick roll in the hay?

He could see how it might look. But surely she knew Nick was not like that, even if *he* was.

He might not be able to reassure her about his own intentions, but he could at least defend Nick. "Your dad—Nick—is a good man. If he'd known your mom was pregnant, he'd have done his best to make it right."

"I know." She lifted one shoulder. "I'll go get that shower, if it's okay."

"Of course. The eggs should be done in around twenty minutes."

As she walked away, he wondered if he hadn't done such a good job at hiding after all. Because despite all the hard work he'd gone to last night, she seemed to know exactly who—and what—he was.

Kate was on her third day of observations. Laisse had gotten permission not only for her to explore their treatment methods but had handed her a form that would let her apply for an internship. It seemed her training in the States would be valid in the UK, with a bit of tweaking and the addition of a course or two. Nick had finished his therapy so she wouldn't get to help with it as she'd hoped, but they were getting to know each other a little better so she didn't need an excuse to see him.

As she watched the therapist direct a patient on the leg-press machine, she thought about where she and Nick would go from here.

Tiggy, after the initial awkwardness, had been wonderfully accepting of her. She and Nick were obviously deeply in love. She could see it in the way the other woman touched him repeatedly, and the way Nick's ruggedly handsome face softened whenever he looked at his wife. Although he received quite a few sideways looks from other women, he never gave them a second glance. He only had eyes for his wife.

What would it be like to have someone love you so completely that anyone else became invisible? Kate had had boyfriends and lovers, but none of them had scratched below the surface of her heart.

Her mind went to Luke, and she gave an internal headshake. Not in a million years would she go that route.

That man knew women. Intimately. It showed in the way he touched her, the way he could keep her on the cusp of an orgasm without actually letting her tumble over the edge. That only came with experience. Lots of it.

Was that why he seemed to get such pleasure out of watching her reactions? Was he sorting and categorizing her every whimper to have fresh material for whatever new woman crossed his path?

He oozed confidence—was the epitome of self-control. They both knew there would be another woman after her…and others after that.

Like her mother and her letters.

She swallowed. Her dad had loved her mom so very completely, would continue to love her memory no matter what he found out about her.

And as much as she loved him, she did not want to wind up like that. In love with someone who would leave her mourning his loss—even if that loss was emotional rather than physical. The loss that came when he inevitably moved on to the next girl in line.

Did Luke have some kind of secret addiction? She'd heard of there being such a thing, but wasn't sure if it was genuine or simply an excuse for bad behavior. Did Luke have a twisted need to go through woman after woman? Or was he just a shallow playboy?

She'd never gotten that impression from him. Not really. But then again, would her dad have married her mom knowing what was in her past? Knowing the fields of shattered hearts she'd left in her wake?

He might have. But *she* wouldn't. She couldn't.

Someone calling her name made her blink and look up with a start.

Tiggy frowned down at her. Judging from her nurse's uniform, she was working today. "So sorry. I didn't mean to frighten you."

"You didn't. I was just daydreaming."

The other woman smiled. "It's quite all right. I was on a break and decided to come by and see if you were here. Too bad Nick isn't still in therapy."

"Don't be. I'm glad he's fully recovered. He was very lucky, from what I understand. If he'd waited much longer to have the surgery…" She let her sentence trail away.

"Yes, he was lucky." Tiggy dropped into the chair next to hers. "And I'm a lucky woman to have him."

There it was again. The evidence of their love. Kate was happy for them but more certain than ever that what Tiggy and Nick had was rare.

"Did you and Luke know each other in the States?"

It was as if the other woman knew he'd been on her mind. "No. I met him here in London."

"He called me, you know, after Nick was admitted. He's part of the reason we're back together."

"I didn't know that." Kate touched her hand. "I know it's been awkward having me around…knowing I'm

Nick's daughter. I'm really sorry for showing up un-
announced."

"We would have had to work through things eventually. You just hurried it along a bit." The corners of
her eyes crinkled as she smiled and rubbed her abdomen. "I'm glad you're here. I want the baby to know
his or her big sister."

Kate sucked in a quick breath, a wave of emotion
rolling through her. The backs of her eyes prickled,
and she blinked to keep the sensation from morphing
into actual moisture. "Thank you so much. I expected
you to want…" She tried to figure out what to say and
finally settled for, "Thank you for including me. I'm
so very grateful."

"You're a part of our lives now. Mine and Nick's."

Tiggy rose to her feet with another smile. "I should
head back to work. But I'll see you later."

As Kate watched her walk away, a pang of envy
went through her. She shook it off with a new sense of
determination.

Someday. *Someday.* That was the kind of relationship
she hoped to find with a man. Until then she wouldn't
settle for less. She gave a rueful grin. Even if the sex
was out of this world.

CHAPTER FIFTEEN

"Is it broken?"

The child who sat cradling her right arm on the steel table in the exam room couldn't be older than four or five.

Luke glanced at the mother, who perched on a chair near the door, hands gripping the bottom of the seat. She looked like she might fly away at any second. She repeated her question. "Macy's arm? Is it broken?"

He tried to keep his mind on the situation at hand, but all he could hear was Kate's quiet request. *I'd like them unbroken.*

In trying to protect himself, he could end up hurting her badly, if he wasn't careful. And as soon as he got off tonight he was going to call her and let her know he wouldn't be bothering her anymore.

Thankful he wasn't dealing with a compound fracture—where the bone pushed through the skin—he laid a hand on the child's head to reassure her. "I'll need to get an X-ray, but I'd say there's a good possibility that this bone right here—" he ran his fingers along the outside of his own forearm "—the ulna, is broken. What happened?"

Her mother spoke up. "She was riding her bike and fell against a brick wall."

Had she answered a bit too quickly? He glanced down at the child and examined the skin around the injury. "That must have hurt." The area wasn't scraped, as he'd expect after contact with a wall, but there was quite a bit of bruising. "Do you hurt anywhere else?"

The child's glance went to her mother, and then she looked at her shoes—dingy white sneakers that dangled three feet off the floor. She shrugged a too-thin shoulder.

Something about this scenario stuck a familiar chord. Dread crowded his chest.

Luke frowned and took a closer look at the mother. Nervous. Shoulders slumped, a permanent curve to the back of her neck, as if she'd been beaten down her whole life. "Did she mention anything to you?"

"I didn't see her fall. She rode home and said her arm hurt."

"She got back on her bicycle after hurting her arm?" That didn't seem likely. The child was four. Where had the mother been?

"I think so. I didn't see it."

He forced a smile and looked back down at the girl. "I used to skin my knees or scrape my palms when I fell off my bike. Do your knees hurt?" The child's palms were as clean as a whistle. No abrasions from trying to stop her fall. The child said nothing, so he looked back at the mom, brows raised in question.

"She fell off her bike." The mother's hand went to her own cheek, in a kind of cupping motion that sent a chill down Luke's spine. His sense of foreboding grew.

The story didn't waver, no hint of asking her daughter for any kind of clarification. She was hiding something. About her daughter's accident…and behind her hand.

The woman's fingers stayed where they were, her

elbow resting on her knee in a casual gesture that was made to look like she was propping herself on it.

What was she hiding? And why the hell hadn't he looked at her more closely when he'd come into the room?

Because you forgot. Grew complacent. And the urge to hide things never quite went away.

He tried again, this time keeping an eye on the mother as he directed another question at Macy. "Did someone push you off your bike?" He gave her a reassuring smile that he hoped didn't look as scary as it felt. "Or hurt you in some other way?"

The mother was off her chair in a flash, just like he'd known she would be. And he got a better look at that cheek.

"I already told you, she fell off her bike."

He ignored the words, knowing they were a lie even as his eyes traveled over the woman's face. *Dammit.* Beneath a thick smear of beige makeup he caught a glimpse of purple skin. Her fingers were already back at the spot, moving back and forth as if scratching an itch that just wouldn't fade.

How many of those itches had she scratched over the years?

How many lights had she turned off so no one would see what she'd hidden from the world? Pretending normalcy where there was none?

He brushed away the thought before it took hold.

This is not about you, Blackman. Get your head back in the game.

"What happened to your cheek?" He knew better than try to pull her hand away and force her to admit the truth.

"M-my cheek? Nothing." She licked her lips, her

hand going back to cover the spot, no longer trying to make it appear casual. "It's just a rash. I get them sometimes."

I bet you do.

"Let me take a look. Maybe I can do something about it."

"No!" She moved away from him a pace or two before the backs of her knees hit the chair, and she went down with a plop. "It's eczema. I already have medicine for it."

How many lies did that make so far?

The last thing he wanted was for her to turn combative, though, and drag her daughter out of the room with a possible bone fracture. "It's okay. We'll just need to send Macy for an X-ray to see what's going on."

"I want to go with her."

"Of course you do." He picked up a phone. "Let me call and have them send someone down for her."

"O-okay." She twisted her hands in her lap. "I want to go with her."

The words were almost a whisper this time, and Luke wondered if it was a mother's silent plea not to be separated from her child.

Maybe so. But he couldn't dredge up much more sympathy for her than he'd had toward his own mother, who'd let her husband pound on her—and him—when he'd tried to step in between them. She'd never once tried to stop him from intervening.

Had little Macy done the same? Stepped in front of her father's fists, only to have him strike out at her instead? If she'd lifted a hand to ward off a blow, this was exactly the type of fracture that might have occurred.

He put in a call to Claire Mathers, the hospital administrator, who picked up right away.

"This is Dr. Blackman. I have a little girl down here around four years old with a possible fractured ulna. I need an X-ray and a consult." He said it with just enough emphasis that Claire would understand what he was saying.

It was one of the things he'd insisted on when he'd come to the hospital, that he have a way of reporting possible child abuse cases without raising alarms. He knew from experience that mothers did sometimes drag their children away from much-needed medical care if they feared they were about to be discovered. Claire had told him to call her, and she'd take it from there, alerting the authorities before the mother had a chance to take off.

"Just keep her there for a few minutes, and I'll send for someone."

"Thanks. Let us know when they're ready for her in X-Ray."

The mother settled back down in her chair, her chest rising in a sigh of relief. "It won't take long, will it?"

"Shouldn't be more than fifteen or twenty minutes." He wasn't leaving the room until Claire arrived. Glancing around the sterile white walls, hoping to find something to take the girl's mind off her pain, he came up empty. He'd have to go back to the old blow-up-the-surgical-glove trick. He drew one from a nearby dispenser, blew it up and handed it to the child, who gave her first tentative smile. He glanced at the mother again. "Is there anyone you'd like me to call? Macy's father, perhaps?"

She shook her head, settling deeper in her chair, her hand no longer covering her injury. "We're divorced."

"How about you? Do you want someone here with you while you wait? If Macy's arm is broken, it could be a while before they can set it. Your mother?" He paused, then said, "How about a boyfriend?"

A spot of color appeared along the woman's left cheekbone—the makeup and bruising hiding anything on the other side. "My boyfriend isn't home right now."

Otherwise she wouldn't be here with Macy. Another puzzle piece dropped into place.

"I see."

On impulse, he squatted beside her and looked into blue eyes that appeared just as washed out and hopeless as the rest of her. His mother had had that same look at times. That trapped, hopeless, beaten-down facade that hid a wealth of pain. He despised whoever had caused that. And yet by her silence she was resigning her child to the same sad existence.

He touched her hand. "Is there anything you'd like to talk about? We can step outside if you'd like."

A sound like the quick squeak of a child who couldn't see past the needle to the lifesaving vaccine came out of her throat. "No. Macy and I are fine. We're going to be just fine."

Hell. Why couldn't she just admit the truth? A small bead of anger coursed down his spine.

"Take a good look at your daughter, and tell me again how fine you are."

She met his eyes, the pain finally out in the open. "He loves us. He does."

How could she even say those words?

His mother had said the same thing. Over and over. He had never been sure if it had been a statement of fact or a prayer.

Luke had wanted no part of that particular cycle. He figured if he had some kind of genetic defect, he was going to turn it on himself and not someone else. He'd engaged in dangerous behaviors that had slowly escalated over the years. Going from merely reckless, to possibly deadly—as he'd found out during that knife fight.

Maybe his leg injury had been part of that quest to save others by harming himself. And just like this mother, he hid his scars from everyone. Even himself.

He stood to his feet, feeling defeated. She wasn't going to come out and admit the person she was with was an asshole, any more than his mother had.

Well, if she wouldn't do this the easy way then he hoped the authorities saw past the lies and took Macy out of that home before something much more valuable than her arm was broken. Maybe it would even shock the girl's mother into getting the help she seemed to desperately need.

"Will they be doing Macy's X-ray pretty soon?"

"I hope so."

Come on, Claire. She's getting spooked.

Just then there was a knock on the door and the administrator herself appeared, along with an orderly pushing a wheelchair.

"Hello, Dr. Blackman. Is this your patient?" Claire, her short dark hair dancing around an elfin face, glanced at him for confirmation. She smiled, looking as sweet as pie, but beneath the cheerful facade was a shark, one who wasn't afraid of taking a chunk out of anyone who deserved it.

He nodded. "Yes, this is Macy." He tweaked the child's hair. "Ms. Mathers is going to take you upstairs to get a picture of your arm."

"We'll just get her into the chair and be on our way."

Luke scribbled the word *Boyfriend* on a sheet of paper on the metal chart holder, handing it to Claire.

The other woman nodded that she understood. Then, before the orderly could move, Luke scooped the little girl into his arms and settled her into the wheelchair, making sure he didn't bump her arm in the process. "They'll get you all patched up."

At least physically. Who could say what kind of scars she'd carry on the inside? His palm scrubbed over his leg as he watched the group go out the door, the mother's frightened eyes glancing one last time at his face.

As soon as they were gone, he dropped into the chair the woman had vacated and dragged a hand through his hair. He felt awful about betraying her, but he'd had no choice. Not only was it the law to report suspected cases of child abuse, it was the right thing to do. He'd never have called Claire if he hadn't been very sure of the warning signs. From what he could see, Macy was being abused, and her mother wasn't able—or willing—to put a stop to it.

Instead, she'd hidden it, much like Luke's parents had hidden what had happened in their household.

All it would take was letting one person see the truth, and the spell would be broken forever. Macy's mom could then leap over the roadblock that kept her imprisoned. But she had to be willing. Once she took that first step it would get easier to take the next one...and the next.

He frowned. Wasn't he doing the same thing with his scars? He hid them even from himself. Why? Because if he didn't acknowledge they existed, he could pretend his life was normal.

Like Macy's mother did each and every day?

He'd been perfectly willing to stand there and lecture her, all the while knowing he was no better than she was.

Maybe he should follow his own diagnosis. Maybe it was time to let at least one person—besides his medical providers—in on his secret. But how on earth was he going to do that?

He could leave the lights on the next time he had a date, and just let the chips fall where they may.

Right. And if he did that with someone at work, he'd have to face them again day in and day out. No, he'd rather it be with someone outside the hospital. Someone he wasn't afraid would flinch away in disgust or coo with pity as soon as she got a good look at his reality.

Kate's image came to mind, the way she'd asked him to leave the lights on. And she'd already seen a good portion of his leg during that massage she'd given him.

Take that first step. Just like you urged Macy's mother to do. You can do it.

He took a steadying breath and tried to think. Kate had brushed away his arguments and hadn't made a single sound when she'd slid that towel up—not high enough to see the worst of the damage but enough that she had a pretty good idea what was there. And she had to have seen the difference in size between his legs.

And yet she'd slept with him, anyway. Had whimpered his name. Had wanted the lights on.

Even as he told himself it was crazy, he stood, wondering if Kate was still over in the physical therapy wing. They wouldn't have sex. He'd just take her to the nearest safe place and let her see the truth. Not for her sake but for his. He could—and would—expose who he really was once and for all.

CHAPTER SIXTEEN

KATE PICKED UP her purse and headed for the door, waving at Laisse. The crew at the rehabilitation center had been wonderful. They were doing an excellent job with their patients. And it was interesting to see the different techniques used here.

"You're coming back tomorrow?" Laisse asked.

"If it's okay."

"Of course it is. Maybe we can have lunch together."

Kate nodded, giving the woman a smile. "I'd love that. Thanks again for everything."

"Anytime, love."

She smiled at the ready expression and pushed through the door, turning left to head toward the exit. A hand wrapped around her arm, halting her progress and ripping a squeaked sound of alarm from her throat.

"Hey, what the—?"

Whirling round, her breath caught when she saw Luke standing there. He'd made no attempt to see her for the past three days, and she'd assumed that was how he wanted it.

She took one look at his face and said, "Is everything okay?"

"Yes. Have you got a few minutes?"

"Of course. I was just headed back to the hotel. Do you want to come?"

He hesitated then shook his head. "Better if I don't."

She knew exactly why. It was dangerous. For both of them. At least Luke was honest enough to admit it. "Is your leg bothering you?"

"Yes. No." He scrubbed a hand down the back of his neck. "I'm not even sure why I'm here, other than I just had a rough case. It made me think."

"About?"

"About my past. About my current attitudes."

Kate wasn't sure what he was talking about, but he had a reason for seeking her out. She just needed to give him some space to get there. So she nodded. "How can I help?"

"Actually, I need to show you something."

"All right." She waited, figuring he was going to pull something out of his pocket or something, but he just stood there. She prodded him. "Do you want to show me here?"

He gave a quick laugh and glanced at the window, where Laisse was watching them with curious eyes. "I think that might get me arrested."

"Excuse me?" What on earth could he want to show her that was…? Well, she could think of one thing, but he'd already said he didn't want to go to her hotel room. She assumed that meant he didn't want to have sex with her. Which was fine by her.

His fingers were working his leg again, something he did regularly.

"Does it have to do with that?" She nodded at it.

He immediately shoved his hand into his pocket. "You asked about the lights several nights ago. And I wanted to show you why I didn't want them on."

"You want to show me your leg?"

"Yes."

Never in a million years would she have guessed that's what he wanted. "Can you tell me why?"

He dragged a hand through his hair. "I have no idea, really, except the case I mentioned a few minutes ago involved a child with a broken arm. I could tell her mother was hiding something. I think her boyfriend hit both of them and she's covering for him. All I could think about was that if she would just tell one person the truth, she could break the cycle."

"How awful. I'm sorry."

He waved away her sympathy. "Maybe I'm doing the same thing with my leg." A beat went by. "You're not going to be here much longer, and you've already seen part of it, so I thought... I want to see if I can get past this."

A sliver of hurt went through her. She was safe. Temporary. Of course she was the logical candidate. She was a physical therapist, used to seeing wounds of all shapes and sizes. She'd be leaving soon, and the implication was that he had no intention of trying to prolong their relationship once she got on that plane.

And she realized she'd actually harbored some kind of twisted hope that he *would* want to. That he might not be who she feared he was: a playboy, who hopped from one relationship to another.

She should put her plan of steering clear of him into action.

Except if she did so right now and refused his request, he was bound to take it the wrong way, maybe even think she was too disgusted by the thought to agree.

She already knew what she was going to say. Yes.

Just like she always did when it came to Luke. "Would you rather do it here than at your house? That's a long way to drive."

"I think you'd agree the supply closet doesn't have the best track record."

Neither did her hotel room. Or his apartment, for that matter. In fact, no place seemed to be safe.

As if aware of her thoughts, he said, "This isn't some ploy to get you back in bed." His quick grin looked pained. "I can think of better ways to do that."

Oh, he could, could he? "You seem pretty sure of yourself."

"Am I wrong?"

No, damn him. He wasn't wrong. And she was afraid that just by agreeing to go to his house, she was going to prove that once and for all. "What about your case?"

"I've handed it over to the hospital administrator. If she needs me to give a statement, she'll call me. I've already told her I might be out of the hospital for a while." He studied her for a few seconds, his lips thinning. "Listen, forget it. I'm sure you have other things to do. Like visit Nick."

Before she had a chance to open her mouth, he swung away, striding down the hall with that half swagger, half limp that tugged at her heartstrings. She couldn't bear him to think she was rejecting him, and she couldn't tell him the real reason…that she was terrified of her growing feelings.

She should just let him go. Instead, she hurried to catch up with him before he had a chance to disappear around the corner. She grabbed at his hand. "I want to."

He stopped but didn't look down at her. "You want to what?"

Kate swallowed. "Look at your leg. And anything else you might want me to do."

Luke gritted his teeth, forcing himself to stay put as Kate propped herself on her elbow, fingers trailing up the bare skin of his damaged leg. The curtains were wide open, and light invaded the room from all angles. There was a bed sheet within reach and habit made him want to yank it over himself, but he didn't.

She continued what she was doing, carefully following the ragged dips and grooves that marked where the explosive blasts had caught him, where the surgeons' scalpels had left their own distinctive marks as they'd done their best to make sense of the macerated muscle and sinew left behind.

And where they hadn't been able to find enough skin to cover the damage, they'd harvested pieces from the back of his uninjured hip. Kate had found each and every injury and had touched it. With her hands. With her mouth.

He'd been blown away. Sensations he couldn't even define had rocketed through him, tearing away what he *thought* he knew just as surely as the metal shrapnel had sliced through his leg and hip. What she'd done to him had created an amalgamation of lust and fear. Even now the urge to switch off the lights was almost overpowering.

But it was already too late. He'd let one person see the truth. And see him she had. She'd made love to him beneath the glare of the overhead lights—taking the lead this time. He couldn't remember the last time a woman had done that, although the fault for that lay entirely with him.

He was thoroughly sated—and yet there was a deep

well of need within him that wanted more. Wanted her. If the mind-over-matter school of thought really was true, Kate would be flat on her back again in a matter of seconds.

"Tell me about it." Her quiet voice broke through his thoughts, even as she continued to explore his leg. She was as naked as he was, and he drew a small measure of comfort from that. He could bet she'd remained that way on purpose, just to make him feel better.

And he did. He leaned over and pressed his lips to her bare shoulder, breathing in her scent. Their combined scents.

It was heady, and he didn't want to think about why that reached beneath his skin and touched something deep inside him.

He leaned back. "What do you want to know?"

"Everything." Her eyes met his. "How you were injured. What kinds of therapy you had."

Luke wasn't sure he wanted to relive those terrifying minutes leading up to his injury. In fact, a lot of the aftermath was fuzzy. But his purpose in dragging her back to his house had been to let someone see the truth. To know that he was capable of exposing it once and for all.

So he took a deep breath. "My commanding officer had received reports of insurgents, along with some possible injuries, so my company was sent on a reconnaissance mission. We were to meet up with British troops at the designated location. We weren't supposed to engage, just report our findings."

Her fingers paused and her palm curved over his thigh in an almost possessive gesture that made something twist inside him.

"Where was this?" she asked.

"In Afghanistan, ten years ago." He lay back against the pillows, threading his fingers behind his head. "We didn't know we were walking into a trap. I was hit, and Nick saved my life and my leg. That's about it."

Her brows went up. "You win the prize for the shortest explanation of an injury ever."

He laughed. "Just sticking to the facts, ma'am."

"Hmm." Her palm slid a few centimeters higher. And it seemed his brain actually did wield some power over his body because things shifted. "Did your surgery happen in the field?"

"No. They stabilized me and then shipped me off to Germany to do the biggest chunk of repairs, and then on to Walter Reed for the rest of it."

"You received a medical discharge."

She didn't even need to ask. His leg told her all that and more. "Yes."

"Were you a doctor in the military?"

"No, that came afterward." This subject was a little trickier. "After I heard about what Nick did, how he fought to save my leg, even when other people were telling him it was a lost cause, it made me want to do the same for others. The emergency room is basically a glorified triage unit."

"And you save lives."

"Not always." He remembered that accident victim he and Kate had encountered on their way back from the restaurant. That seemed like a lifetime ago. And he'd had no idea that agreeing to do Nick a favor would end up with Kate lying in his bed, hearing confessions he'd told no one.

"You helped that little girl today."

He'd filled Kate in on Macy and his suspicions about the boyfriend on the way to his house. "Who knows whether I made any difference at all? She might end up back at the emergency room with another injury in a couple of days. A couple of months."

Hell, he hoped not. Because he'd sure be tempted to take matters into his own hands at that point.

Although the guy could probably beat the living daylights out of him. Or send him toppling onto his ass with one good shove. But he'd be willing to give it a try. Surely he could get one or two good punches in before the other guy took him down. Then again, maybe the guy wouldn't bother sticking around. His dad had hightailed it out of the house at the first sign of police involvement. He had only been big and powerful around his wife and child, who'd lived in terror of his temper.

"If the mother knows the hospital is suspicious, maybe she'll make an effort or kick the guy out."

"Or maybe she's just the type of woman who jumps from loser to loser, as if she can't get enough." His breath came out in a rough snort. "I just don't understand not caring enough about your kid to find a good man and stick with him."

Kate's teeth came down on her lip, digging hard. A flicker of what looked like pain flashed through her eyes and was gone. But when her hand tried to withdraw from his thigh, he put his over it, holding it in place. "What is it?"

"Nothing." Even her voice sounded raw, as if he'd touched on something. But what? She'd been raised in a happy, stable home, from all appearances.

"Then why are you suddenly so fidgety?" He had the feeling she was about to run, and he didn't want her to.

"You said you were good at hiding things. You don't know the meaning of the word."

"I don't understand."

"I didn't know who my real father was until my mom died, remember?"

Damn. He hadn't even thought about that when he'd spouted off his little sob story. He rolled onto his side to face her. "I'm sorry, Kate. But at least Nick's a good man. So is your adoptive father, from what you've said. Your mom didn't go after losers."

"Really? I wouldn't know."

She'd totally lost him now. Was she saying Nick wasn't a good man? Or that her mother had indeed gone after losers?

"Was she with someone who hurt her?" The thought of someone lifting his hand and striking Kate made acid pour into his stomach, turning it sour.

"Again, I wouldn't know. There were so many of them."

"There were so many what? Men?" His fingers curled around hers, still afraid she was going to bolt at any second.

"Yes." She nodded, not quite meeting his eyes. "There were evidently lots of them. And I had no idea."

"But if they all happened before you were born, before she met your dad, I don't understand why you're—"

"I'm pretty sure they didn't just happen before she married my dad."

Her hand gripped his tightly, as if she needed some extra support.

"She saw other men while she was married?"

"Yes."

"You said you didn't find Nick's letter until after she died, so how do you know she did?" Could her father have accused her mother of something like that? If so, why?

"Because Nick's letter wasn't the only one I found

in that closet. There were lots of them. Maybe fifty, although I couldn't bring myself to count them." She paused for a long moment. "More than half of them were dated after Mom met my dad. And I'd bet every one of those men knew she was married. So, yes, I know exactly the type of woman who would sleep with loser after loser, even when she had a good man at home. Because that woman was my mother."

CHAPTER SEVENTEEN

YOU'RE NOT GOING to wind up like your mother.

Luke's words—a reaction to her unintended revelation—still echoed in her head two days after their encounter. Oh, the irony of hearing them while sprawled on the bed of a man she barely knew. And to have them spoken by a man who'd slept with more than his share of women.

But he'd shown her his scars. Ones he'd hidden from everyone else, evidently. And he'd told her his story. The urge had been there to take him in her arms and kiss all that hurt away, but she'd had a sense that he wouldn't welcome the gesture.

And it was hearing him talk about his fight to regain the use of his leg that had made her realize something terrible. Something that could shatter everything she thought she knew about herself.

She loved him. And it was the last thing she'd ever intended to do. She was here in London for such a short time. Luke's job was here, while hers was back in Memphis. Along with her dad and the rest of her life. She couldn't just pick up and move to England, even if he suddenly asked her to.

Not that he ever would. He'd never given her any indication that he felt something more than simple physical attraction where she was concerned. Yes, their time together had been exciting and crazy, and he turned her on like no man ever had. That was nothing to build a whole life around, though.

But he showed you his scars.

The argument continued to run circles around anything she put forth to counter it. It refused to be swayed or moved by anything she threw at it. And, boy, did she have a whole arsenal up her sleeve.

She fingered a bouquet of white roses in a cut-glass vase. They had arrived yesterday morning, along with a little note.

Thanks for last night.
L.B.

L.B. Luke Blackman.

She wasn't exactly sure what he was thanking her for. Sex? For allowing him to drag her home and participate in a very revealing show-and-tell session? Well, the latter hadn't been much of a hardship. The man was pure chiseled muscle. Yes, his leg and hip were terribly scarred, but those scars didn't take away from his sizzling masculinity. They simply brought him back down to earth. Close enough that she could touch him. All of him.

And, boy, had she ever. There'd been something heady…almost taboo about the experience. Maybe because she knew not many women—if any—had ever got to experience that degree of intimacy with him. And in all honesty he'd come on so strong during their other lovemaking sessions that she hadn't been able to catch her breath long enough to care about what she had and hadn't seen.

She sat down in a chair and gazed at the petals of the flowers in front of her.

Perfect. Just like that night had been.

There had been something intensely personal about her mouth surrounding him. That he hadn't expected it was obvious. His quick gasp of surprise, followed by a hand shoving deep into her hair and closing around the loose strands—and those razor-edged seconds when she'd wondered if he might use his grip to pull her away—had been followed by a raw groan of acceptance...and need. That memory was seared in her brain.

He'd let her take him. Had handed over the reins and allowed her to pleasure him in whatever way she wanted. And she had. She'd done everything she'd ever dreamed of doing.

A shiver went over her, her nipples puckering when her mind flashed through several graphic images in quick succession, like a seductive slide show.

Whew. It had been like a fantasy come true.

But that's all it was. A fantasy. She would be leaving soon. She'd been putting off booking her return flight. She wasn't sure why, but she was eventually going to have to face the fact that the fairy-tale visit had come to an end. She'd go back into hibernation and forget what had happened here.

She hoped.

Nick had called that morning and asked her to come over and look at plans for their nursery. It was hard to believe she was going to be a half sister.

She'd called the physical therapy department at the hospital and told them she wouldn't be coming in today. Laisse seemed disappointed, especially when Kate mentioned she might be leaving soon. The other woman encouraged her to think it over. They were currently swamped and could use the extra hands—her boss had even mentioned hiring an extra therapist. Laisse had half hoped it might be Kate. They were already checking into the certification requirements.

It was sweet of her, but how uncomfortable would that be, working at the same hospital as Luke? She had to imagine things would be strained, especially if she saw him going out with another nurse—or any other woman, for that matter.

No, it was probably better to just head home and lick her wounds in private, not that Luke had led her on in any way. Besides, her father needed her now more than ever. She made a mental to call Luke after she got back from Nick's.

She stood and went over to her suitcase, looking for something to wear. As happy as she was for Nick and Tiggy, she found herself having to work up some genuine enthusiasm for the outing. Because what she wanted more than anything was to hear that phone ring and have it be Luke asking her out. Asking her to consider staying for a while longer. But other than the flowers and Nick, that phone had been totally silent. And so had she. Even Nick had noticed her disappointment when it had been him calling and not Luke. But she'd put on her happy voice and said she'd be thrilled to come over. He'd seemed to accept it. Then again, he was probably lost in his own world right now with the baby and everything else.

Finally deciding on a pair of beige slacks and a green wrap top, she tossed the clothes on the bed and went to take a quick shower. She wrapped herself in a towel and applied her makeup with a careful hand, trying to control the slight tremor of doom that seemed to have come out of nowhere. A half hour later, she was dressed, with her hair blow-dried to fall straight around her shoulders.

Just as she picked up her purse, ready to head to the lobby, the bedside phone rang. Her heart pounded in her chest as she picked it up, which was ridiculous. It was probably just Nick, asking if she was on her way.

"Hello?"

"Ms. Bradley?"

She sighed when she recognized the voice of the lady from the hotel reception desk. "Yes?"

"Mr. Blackman is downstairs. Do you want me to send him up?"

He was here? At the hotel? She couldn't hold back a huge smile. How much better was this than a phone call?

Okay, so did she let him come up?

Absolutely not. She might be a glutton for punishment but she hoped she hadn't reached the masochist stage yet. "Would you mind telling him I'll be right down?"

"Certainly."

She dropped the phone back on its cradle and took one more quick glance in the mirror, exhilaration giving way to nerves. Well, it was now or never.

The elevator doors opened and Luke swallowed when Kate walked out. Her normally wavy hair was now straight, with just the slightest hint of curve at the ends. The top she wore skimmed her breasts, some kind of tie wrapping just beneath them, which she'd knotted at the side. Man, did his fingers itch to pull one end of that string and see what happened.

He pushed away from the counter and went over to greet her, keeping his hands by his sides.

"Thank you for the flowers," she blurted when he got close. "But there was no need."

"I thought there was." He kept his voice low enough that only she could hear. He'd wanted to give them to her in person—as an excuse to see her again—but she hadn't been at the hospital. He'd resisted the urge to come over after work last night. Then he'd got Nick's call, mentioning that Kate was coming over to look at the nursery and asking if he wanted to, as well. It had given him the perfect excuse to come to the hotel.

She searched his face, as if looking for something and not finding it. "I was just getting ready to go to Nick's."

"I thought you might be. I stopped to see if you might want a ride."

"You know about…?" She slung her purse over her shoulder and crossed her arms. "You're going to his house as well, aren't you?"

"He called this morning and asked if I'd like to."

An expression of wariness passed through her eyes that made his muscles tense up. Did she think he was just trying to sleep with her every chance he got?

His glance went to the tie on her shirt again and he tightened his lips. Okay, so even *he* wasn't sure of his motives. Not good. "Since I'm here, we may as well ride together."

"I guess so."

His lips curved. If he'd expected her to lunge for him the second she saw him and wrap her arms around his neck, he could pretty much bet that wasn't going to happen. But that was good, right? Because he had to somehow get across that he planned on retreating to his customary fallback position—casual acquaintances, where he hoped they could remain until she left to go back to the States.

Waiting until she'd buckled herself into the car seat, he turned the ignition key and eased onto the street in front of the hotel. She sat stiffly with her hands folded in her lap, fingers twined.

He pulled his attention back to the road. "So what did you do today? I didn't see you at the hospital."

"No. I decided to stick close to the hotel. Went for a run. Caught up on the news."

He frowned, hands tightening on the wheel. "That's right. I forgot you're a runner. Have you had any more problems with your admirer from last week?"

"Who...? Oh, the surfer-type guy? I think he's already checked out. And he wasn't my admirer."

"No, just someone who wanted to be your new jogging buddy." He couldn't quite keep the bitter acid from rising in his throat and coloring his words.

She turned sideways. "Luke, is something wrong? I'm not really sure why you came to pick me up. Just because we slept together it doesn't mean you have to send flowers or take me places. I get it. This is a temporary fling, and we both know it. I'm not pushing for more, if that's what you're afraid of."

"That's definitely not what I'm afraid of."

"Then what is it?"

He wrapped his hand around the knob of the stick shift, letting the lever slide between his index and middle fingers as he put the car into third gear. The act gave him time to consider his answer. "After we leave Nick's, I'd like to talk to you. Maybe before we get back to the hotel."

Her eyes grew wary. "That's not necessary. I think I can guess what this is about."

She really couldn't. Because even he didn't know exactly what he meant to say. All he knew was that for the past two days he'd been at war with himself. Part of him said this girl was something special and he'd better hang on to her. And that part of him was spoiling for a fight. Because the other part of him, the part that said she needed someone who could fight for her—literally—said he needed to limp away from her as fast as he could.

He'd already done something he'd never done with a woman before: let her see him in all his battered, twisted glory. And he still had no idea why. Not really. It had been a reaction to his child abuse patient, but looking back at it he realized how utterly stupid that reasoning was. Yes, he was hiding something, but he wasn't hurting anyone in the process, except maybe himself. And he'd been able to deal with it for the past ten years.

Hadn't he?

He shook off the thoughts and tried to answer her. "I don't want you to the get the wrong idea."

"Believe me, I'm not."

Okay, he was messing this up big time. "That's why I wanted to wait until we left Nick's. So we could sit and talk like rational human beings."

"I think I'm being perfectly rational. I never thought we were an item. Not once. So don't worry about it."

Well, good. He could relax now. So why did his spine feel like it had been replaced by a length of cold, hard pipe?

There was nothing he could do about it now, though, because they were about a block away from Nick's place. And they somehow needed to get through that visit without Nick figuring out something was wrong.

"Look. Let's just visit Nick, ooh and ahh over his kid's new digs and then get out of there."

Her lips curved, her frown disappearing. "'His kid's new digs'? You make it sound like they're outfitting a bachelor pad or something. The baby might be a girl."

A daughter. He could picture what Kate's little girl might look like, if she ever had one. Creamy blond hair, big blue eyes, a smattering of freckles across her nose. And he would no more be able to dance with her than he would with her mother. No father-daughter dances. No camping trips. No soccer games.

But there was one thing he seemed to be really good at: throwing himself the biggest damn pity party known to man. He'd always thought he'd dealt with his disability pretty well.

Until Kate had come along.

He pulled into Nick's garage with a grim determination that things were about to change. He was going to hunt down his soul's AWOL Zen master and put him back on active duty. With a reminder that he still had another fifty or so years of service before he received his discharge papers. And then he'd get his life back on track.

CHAPTER EIGHTEEN

"It's going to be beautiful," Kate said, standing inside the empty room in Nick and Tiggy's house. On the wall were color swatches and myriad fabrics taped beneath various pictures.

She saw Nick and Luke give each other The Look, and knew they had no idea how she could tell enough to even offer an opinion. But she could. Soft green walls and muted cream carpeting would provide a backdrop to various pieces of oak furniture: solid changing table with attached dresser, a carved crib with matching green linens and bumper pads, a cream wallpaper border with images of pastel animals, just above the height of the crib's top rail.

"Isn't it? I think it'll be brilliant."

Kate moved farther into the room and studied a magazine picture of the crib.

"It converts into a toddler bed once the baby's outgrown it."

A pang of envy went through her. She was still young, but the future suddenly stretched ahead of her like a barren wasteland. What if she never met anyone she wanted to share her life with? She wanted children someday. But she didn't want to do it the way her mother had.

Although Kate wouldn't trade her adoptive father for anything. He'd given her love and a safe haven. And now she had a second father figure. Nick may not have been there during her formative years but it was obvious he wanted to be a part of her life now, even though it had been her who'd sought him out. She'd been angry at the time—at him, at her mother, at everyone. But she saw now how silly her attitude had been. Nick had had no say in the matter. He hadn't even known she'd existed.

Kate forced herself to look more closely at the picture. "The railings convert into a headboard and footboard?"

"Exactly." Tiggy brushed her hands over her stomach, her whole demeanor glowing and happy. "It's quite a clever system, actually. You'll have to help me with the arranging once everything arrives in a couple of weeks."

"Oh, uh…" She hadn't thought about how to tell them she'd decided to head back to the States soon. It was doubtful she'd still be in London when the furniture got there. "I'm sure you've already got it set up in your mind." She kept the words vague, not wanting to get into this kind of discussion in front of Luke.

"Some of it, yes. But I don't know where the rocker should go. Or if the changing table should go on the wall beneath the window or next to the crib." She glanced at the wall in question. "Where would you put it if you were outfitting a room for your baby?"

Her baby?

Against her will, her eyes slid to Luke's and she noticed a strange heat in his gaze as he stared back—pupils darkening. She swallowed, her mind racing like crazy through all the possibilities. Then Nick broke the spell with the suggestion that the two of them go off for a drink in the den. Once they were gone she allowed herself to sag against the wall, trying her best to make it look casual, even though her legs were shaking. The look Luke had given her had been almost proprietorial, as if any child she might conceive would belong to him as well.

She drew in a slow, careful breath. "I think you're right. I'd want to see the furniture first before I made any firm decisions. Maybe once it arrives you'll know immediately where all of it should go.

"Which is why I want you here." Tiggy smiled. "I don't think Nick quite knows what to make of all this."

Kate tried to deflect Tiggy's attention from dates and turn it back onto the subject of her husband. "He seems really happy."

"We both are, I think." She stared at the door through which Nick had disappeared. "He didn't want children for a long time, you know." She gave Kate a quick hug. "I'm so happy he'll have two now."

"Nick has been really nice about all of this."

"That's the type of man he is. I'm quite partial to him."

Tears pricked Kate's eyelids. Did Tiggy realize how fortunate she was to have found someone like Nick? She thought she probably did.

"Let's go into the kitchen and I'll brew us some tea." She paused. "Or would you rather have coffee?"

"Tea would be wonderful."

"I have black, but I'm trying to stick to herbal during my pregnancy. I do miss my breakfast tea, though."

Once the water was hot, they sat at a small dinette table. Kate tipped milk from a little pitcher into a delicate china teacup, while Tiggy stirred a bit of sugar into her herbal variety. "So how are you enjoying London?" she asked.

"It's a beautiful city. And I love the hospital." And not just the hospital. But now was not the time to think about that. Afraid that Tiggy was going to ask about a date again, she decided to change the subject. "How long did you and Nick know each other before you started dating?"

Tiggy laughed. "Well, that's quite a story. We were attracted from almost the first moment we laid eyes on each other."

The words released a storm in Kate's heart as she remembered the flames that had licked along her veins the first time she'd seen Luke. It hadn't been long afterward they'd wound up in that infamous supply closet.

"How about you? Any boyfriends back home?"

"No, I haven't really had time for one." Which, if Kate really thought about it, was a lie. She just hadn't met someone who was more important than her work. Until now.

And that person had made it perfectly clear he was not the settling-down type. He was right about one thing, though. She was not her mother. She couldn't have a love affair with Luke and then move on to the next man within weeks. She wasn't built like that—even if Luke was. She believed in long-term commitments that endured through the good and bad, whereas Luke didn't even want one that lasted through the good times.

Tiggy touched her hand from across the table. "Someday someone special is going to come along… and you'll know."

"It's a nice thought. But in reality that's not always how it works."

"Not always," Tiggy acknowledged. "And even when it does, a lot of work still has to go into the relationship."

Exactly.

Almost as soon as they finished their tea, Nick and Luke wandered into the room. Nick kissed the top of Tiggy's head, while Luke stood a short distance away, leaning against a nearby wall. She wondered if he was trying to keep some space between them or if his leg was bothering him. When he saw her looking at him, he raised his brows in challenge and purposely shifted his weight onto his injured leg.

Oh, Luke. Haven't you realized you don't have to prove yourself to the world?

"What are you girls talking about?" Nick asked his wife, pulling up a chair and dropping down beside her. He motioned Luke to do the same, but Luke gave a wave of his hand, signifying he was fine where he was.

Heaven forbid he come over and sit by her.

"We were talking about love and how you know when it's real."

A flash of panic shot through Kate's chest. She didn't want Luke to think they'd been talking about the two of them. "Correction. We were talking about how the two of *you* fell in love."

Nick twirled a piece of Tiggy's hair. "We did, didn't we?"

The couple smiled at each other.

Tiggy leaned against her husband's shoulder. "And now we have Kate, as well."

Her eyes went funny for a second, and she had to blink to clear them. The woman who could have slammed the door in her face and told her to never bother them again had instead opened her heart to Kate, as well as her home. She smiled. "Thank you. You both have been so kind. I'm lucky to have not just one wonderful father but two."

Nick leaned back in his chair and scrubbed a hand across the side of his jaw. "Thank you for that. I never dreamed…" He sighed. "Luke said he'd be able to change your mind about me. I'm grateful he was right."

Luke didn't move, but he shot her a glance from his position by the wall. *Bingo.* He knew exactly what his friend was referring to. And that look was one of pure, unadulterated guilt.

"I didn't do anything," he insisted. Kate wasn't sure if the words were directed at Nick or her.

"I didn't know you were modest, too."

"Nick." There was a warning note to his voice now.

Kate's whole body went numb with shock when she realized the implications.

All that time they'd spent together… Had it all been part of some plan—an attempt to gain her trust and sympathy?

Nick nodded. "You're right. It doesn't matter why she's giving me a chance, just that she is."

Please don't say anything else. Either of you.

Her stomach rebelled as she remembered Luke dragging her to his house and showing her his scars. How he'd given her that sob story about how Nick had saved his life…his leg. What she'd done afterward.

Oh, God. She was a bigger fool than she'd thought.

Luke owed Nick his life…he'd said it himself. He'd do anything for the man. Including sleep with his daughter? Or had that been just a little side benefit?

Her cheeks burned red-hot as the horrible realization grew and took root. Luke had been charming her in his bad-boy way and she'd lapped it right up like a cat with a bowl of cream.

Had it all been an act? Had he lied about knowing who she was as they'd drunk coffee together those first few days? He'd acted like she'd tricked him—that she'd used him to get what she wanted. Maybe it was the other way around. Maybe *she* was the one who'd been tricked.

Luke was watching her closely.

She didn't care. Didn't care what he thought she was thinking about. Maybe he was hoping to score again tonight. No way. If she hadn't been stranded she'd have got the hell out of there and driven back to the hotel, where she'd have the biggest boo-hoo session known to womankind. Then tomorrow she was going to pick herself up and book a flight—the first available—out of London, leaving it far behind.

Along with Luke.

Furious and sick inside, she put on a brave but very fake smile and leaned over to kiss Nick's cheek. "I didn't need coaxing from anyone to see what a good man you are. And I'm incredibly fortunate to have found you. I need to get back to my job in the States so I'll be leaving soon—maybe even tomorrow." She gulped back a sob. "But I'll call you. And I'll expect you to keep me posted on the baby. I want pictures of that nursery when it's finished, and—"

Tiggy interrupted her speech. "I thought you were considering staying for a while longer? At least, I hoped you were."

"I'm sure I'll be back someday." But not until her heart had scabbed over. "Maybe after the baby is born." And after Luke has left London.

"We'd love you to stay with us. We have another bedroom."

"Thank you." She pushed back from the table. "I

really need to get back to the hotel, so I'll get out of your hair."

"Are you sure?" Tiggy's voice sounded uneasy. Leave it to a woman to sense when something was wrong. Really wrong. "Can't you stay a while longer?"

Not unless they all wanted to see what a human fire hose looked like. Because she was going to lose it soon.

"No, I'm sorry. I can take a cab."

Luke took a step toward the table. "I'll take you. I have to go back that way, anyway."

The last thing she wanted to do was sit next to him in that tiny car and listen to him try to explain away Nick's words. But maybe he wouldn't even try.

As soon as he dropped her off, though, she was never going to see Luke Blackman again.

CHAPTER NINETEEN

Luke cursed to himself as he shifted the car into Reverse and backed out of the driveway.

He'd seen the moment her face had closed in on itself, her smile fading as she'd realized what Nick had been saying. It was true. He *had* offered to try to portray his friend in a good light—it's why he'd invited her to dinner that first time. But from that point on, what they'd done together had had nothing to do with Nick.

The need to set her straight burned in his chest, along with an explanation that hung on the tip of his tongue. She'd been horrified by Nick's words—humiliated that *he* might have become involved with her for that reason alone. It was why she'd suddenly decided to pick up and leave London tomorrow, he was sure of it. And that fact burned like bile in the back of his throat.

So why wasn't he turning to her and pleading for her to believe him when he said that sleeping with her had had nothing to do with any promise he'd made to Nick?

And yet he held himself still and kept it all inside him. Even as she gripped her hands tightly in her lap and stared out the windshield as if she was barely holding it together.

Wasn't it better this way? The only reason he'd shown her his scars had been because he'd known she was leaving. How much easier did it make things that she was flying out sooner than expected? And that she'd have no thoughts of coming back to pick up where they'd left off?

Easier? That wasn't the right word, because he wanted her to stay and he had no idea why.

Oh, he had an idea. A good one. But he wasn't about to admit it to himself or anyone else, because he couldn't do anything about it.

Seeing that muscular man standing next to Kate in the lobby of the hotel and seeing the healthy glow in her cheeks had been a game-changer for him. Much like the moment he'd realized that car-accident victim had been suffering from flail chest.

The terrain shifted along with his normal response reflexes.

With every other woman there'd been a gradual period of backing off. He'd slept with them a couple of times then he had suddenly been busier at work, offering to take on longer shifts. Not because he'd been an ass who hadn't been able to stick with any one woman but because he hadn't wanted to deal with the ramifications involved with being in a relationship. Or how his physical limitations might affect any children they might have. His lifestyle was something he'd come to accept, even if it wasn't something he'd label as ideal.

Anyway, his method of easing out of any potential relationships had worked until now. The woman in question either got tired of waiting—thinking his sudden lack of availability meant he was a workaholic who'd be the worst kind of husband imaginable—or she got the hint that he wasn't looking for anything lasting.

He was having a harder time selling that line to his heart right now. But deep inside he knew that allowing things to end right here was what he should do. Kate could have any guy in the world. *Any guy.* Why would she want to be with one who regularly tortured himself with thoughts of what he couldn't do?

Even if by some strange twist she did, the last thing Luke wanted was to be her pet project. To feel like every time he gave the slightest twinge of discomfort she was going to pull out all her tools and go to work on him. He wanted to be her equal, not another patient in a long line of patients. Because he'd end up hiding his pain, which would make him resentful of having to do just that. When he got home, all he wanted to do was relax and let his leg recover from the day's work.

The last thing he'd wanted to do, though, was hurt her. "Are you okay?"

She gave a soft laugh that was so devoid of humor it made him wince. "I will be once I get back in my own environment."

"About what Nick said…" He swallowed hard. "I'm sorry."

There. He'd done it. His apology wasn't meant to confirm Nick's assertion, but he knew Kate would take it that way. And he was going to let it stand.

"Don't be. I knew the score from the very beginning." They pulled up in front of her hotel. "I just never thought you were capable of stooping to that level."

"Kate—"

"Don't." She clicked her door open and stepped out onto the polished cobblestones. Giving him one last hard look, she said, "Goodbye, Luke."

The door slammed, and then she was walking away toward the entrance of the hotel. He shifted into Neutral and stepped on the parking brake, his chest tight and his body poised to get out of the car. Closing his eyes, he took a deep breath. And then another. Before he could change his mind he released the brake, put the car into gear and pulled out of the hotel entrance, knowing it was the last time he would ever see Kate Bradley. The pain was worse than anything he'd experienced with his leg. And there was absolutely nothing he could do to fix it.

Kate got off the plane in Memphis and found her dad there to meet her. The tears she'd banished for the past twenty-four hours suddenly resurfaced, and before she knew it she found her face buried against his familiar chest, his arms coming round her. The slight tremor from his Parkinson's just made her tears fall faster.

"Hey, kiddo. What's wrong?" The alarm in his voice was unmistakable.

She scrubbed her eyes with her forearm. "Just missed you, that's all."

Her dad cupped her chin and tipped it up, looking into her face. "You sure?"

"Yes." She pulled in a deep breath. It was time to leave what had happened in England behind her and get on with her life.

Had her mother's insides cramped each time she'd said goodbye to someone? Or had she just smiled and gone on her way?

Kate would never know the reasons she'd done what she had, but she knew her mother had loved her...just as she'd loved Tim Bradley.

She looped her arm around her dad's waist as she drew him away from the gate and toward the baggage claim area. Banishing the last of her tears, she said, "So how have you been? Have you kept up with your therapy?"

"I have. My doctor is going to try a new treatment regimen."

"That's wonderful. What is it?"

The next hour or so was spent giving her an update on his doctors' appointments and the medication he'd be taking in the near future. Kate forced her mind to absorb every word her father said, knowing that it would keep her from dwelling on things she couldn't change.

She'd half hoped she'd get to Heathrow airport to find Luke waiting for her, telling her she'd been all wrong about him. But his tight apology still rang in her ears, an indictment that had said he was indeed guilty of toying with her in order to plead Nick's case.

"Do you want to go out for dinner, or do you want to go straight home?"

She smiled. Her dad was one of the most selfless people she'd ever known, and she loved him dearly. "Can we do both? I need to shower and change, but I'd love to go out and hear all the news."

"Sure thing, pumpkin. And you can tell me how things went in London."

She'd tell him some of it, but not everything. She'd leave out the broken heart she was currently sporting. Neither would they discuss her mother and that shoebox.

He hadn't mentioned it. Maybe he—like Kate—realized it would do no good to dredge up the past and try to figure out what had gone on in her mother's mind. Her mom had indeed carried some secrets to the grave. Or had tried to. She had a feeling Luke would, as well. Would he ever show his scars to another woman?

Her stomach twisted. Did it matter?

If she was honest with herself, she'd say yes because, despite how much his deception had hurt, she really did wish him well. That meant being honest with himself and whoever he was involved with in the future. He needed to face his past and come to terms with it in order to have a shot at a normal life.

Just like she'd have to come to terms with him. And somehow...*somehow* figure out how to put him—and everything that had gone on between them—in the past, once and for all.

If one more person asked him where Kate was, he was going to blow a gasket.

Why would anyone assume he knew?

Maybe because he did?

He alone had seen the look on Kate's face. Knew what had run through her mind. He was the only one who knew what they'd done together.

And for that he would burn. No need to add any earthly voices to the damning mix.

He turned toward his latest inquisitor—Laisse from the physical therapy center—and pasted on a smile. One that hid the ache in his leg, which had grown over the course of the day. One week and counting, since she'd left. "From what I understood, she had to get back home to her job."

"I'm really disappointed she didn't at least come in to say goodbye. We'd talked about her staying at the center. I even thought she was considering it. She would have been a great addition."

She'd seriously thought about working in London? That dark pit in his heart grew a little larger. At least Nick had no idea what had happened, and he intended to keep it that way.

"I don't know anything about that." He knew his tone was short, not inviting her to share anything else about Kate's plans.

"Did you know she was leaving so soon? It's only been a couple of weeks."

The other woman fell into step beside him, and he forced a sigh of exasperation back down his throat. It had been a killer week, with three drug overdoses and a couple of kids who'd taken the family car for a joy-ride and ended up wrapping it around a streetlight. He didn't think he could handle much more. "She might have mentioned it."

In actuality, she hadn't mentioned much of anything during that car ride back to the hotel. He'd picked up the phone the next afternoon and dialed her number, out of morbid curiosity, but she'd already checked out.

Laisse wasn't the only who hadn't received a good-bye.

He brushed the woman off the best he could and made his way to the front entrance. Hell, why was he suddenly getting that homesick feeling again?

It had nothing to do with missing the United States, though, and everything to do with missing a certain throaty drawl that went straight to his gut.

Yeah, he missed her. So what? He'd missed plenty of women after they'd parted ways.

Hadn't he?

Or was it just Kate?

He stopped outside the double doors of the hospital and leaned against one of the brick entry columns, trying to gather his thoughts. Tonight just might be a drinking night.

That was one way to relieve the ache that went far beyond his mangled limb.

As he pushed off to make his way to his car, a silver coupé pulled up next to him. The passenger window powered down and there inside was the last person he wanted to see.

Nick.

"Thought you might feel like heading to a pub for a drink. Unless you have plans."

Plans. Not likely. He couldn't stomach the thought of going on a date—or anything else—with anyone other than Kate. And she was long gone.

"No plans."

"Great. Get in."

Luke opened the passenger door and slid inside the vehicle, stretching his sore leg out in front of him with a sigh. Felt good to get off it.

"Leg bothering you?"

"Not much. How about your back?"

"Hanging in there." He shifted the car into Drive with a laugh. "Will you look at us? Battered and bruised and neither willing to admit we're any different than we once were."

Luke grunted, but didn't answer. He'd admitted it all right. Each and every day. It was why he'd let Kate walk away, when what he'd really wanted to do was tell her that he...

No use thinking thoughts like that. So he changed the topic. "How's Tiggy doing?"

"Great. I'm one lucky SOB." He glanced over at him. "I heard from Kate a couple of days ago. Thought you might like to know."

The hand farthest from Nick slowly tightened into a fist as he tried to stop himself from demanding to know how she was doing...how she'd sounded over the phone...if she missed him at all. Instead, he said, "Oh?"

"Yep. She sounded kind of off."

"Off? In what way?" He forced his voice to remain

casual. He'd hoped against hope she'd get home and forget about him. Blow him off as some jerk who didn't deserve a second thought—just like the guy from the hotel. "Is her father okay? She said he was in the early stages of Parkinson's."

"Seems so strange to hear someone else being called her father, even though I know I don't have the right to think she might one day call me that."

"I got the idea the whole situation was kind of confusing."

"Her mother had other letters in that shoebox, did you know that?"

"Yes." Which made him feel like even more of a dick in not trying to explain that he'd been genuinely attracted to her. That the time they'd spent together had had nothing to do with any favor for Nick. "She told me."

Nick pulled over to the side of the road in front of a pub called The Grill. As Luke stepped on his leg, he realized he probably should have headed straight home. The car ride over had made the muscles stiff, and they were now protesting at being made to go back to work.

"Why aren't you using a cane?"

He tightened his jaw and forced his gait to steady back out. "Don't need one. Besides, patients aren't thrilled about seeing their doctor hobble around the E.R. with a walker."

It was Friday night and the place was hopping. Only these voices sounded animated and hopeful, not those of the beaten-down drunks he'd hoped to find. The last thing he wanted to do was find himself surrounded by revelers.

Because he had nothing to celebrate.

They ventured into the dim recesses of the place and

found a table right away, by some miracle. Luke looked at the drinks menu. He needed something strong. He could always leave his car at the hospital and take a cab back to his apartment.

"I'll have a whiskey, straight."

Nick went to the bar, returning with Luke's whiskey and a Perrier and a glass of ice for himself. When Luke frowned at him, he said, "Someone has to be the designated driver."

Suspicion flared in the back of his mind. What the hell? He'd thought his friend had been looking for a drinking partner.

"Tough day?" Nick leaned back in his seat. "Tiggy said you've been looking a little worse for the wear the last few days."

That's right. He'd noticed her pop by his wing a couple of times. She'd given a little wave and then she'd been off again. Nick's wife seemed pretty shrewd— had she figured something out? Like the fact that he and Kate had been a little more friendly than he'd tried to portray?

Luke tossed back his whiskey and swallowed, welcoming the heat as it burned its way down his esophagus and hit the floor of his stomach. "Now, what's this all about?"

Nick poured his water over the glass of ice and took a drink. "I wanted to ask you a question."

That's what he was afraid of. "Shoot."

"Okay. That night you and Kate came over to dinner I could have sworn there was something cozy going on between you."

"*Cozy.* That's a hell of a word."

"Better than the one that originally came to mind."

Yeah, it probably was. "She's an attractive woman. It'd be hard for any man not to notice."

"I'm assuming this went beyond 'noticing.'"

"Are you asking if I slept with her?"

The other man's jaw tightened. "I'm asking if you care about her."

The shot hit him right between the eyes. He could have fended off a question about his sex life, but this was his friend. Kate's father. A man who'd saved his life. He deserved the truth.

He took a second sip of his whiskey and tried to formulate words. "Yes, I cared about her. A little more than I probably should have."

"How so?"

"I let things go further than I should have, let's just put it that way."

"But not so far that she felt the need to stay."

Luke smiled. "She thinks it was all a set-up, remember? That I did it to beef up your image."

"Damn. That's what I was afraid of." Nick propped his arms on the table in front of him. "I'll call her and set her straight."

"No. Don't. It's better this way."

"You said you cared about her." Nick's eyes zeroed in on his face.

"That doesn't mean I want her to come back over here expecting something I can't give her."

"Like what?"

"A ring. A chance for a normal life." That's exactly what he wanted to do. But it was impossible.

"Normal meaning…"

Luke pushed back in his seat with a rough laugh. "Meaning a guy who can keep up with her." He paused, not sure exactly how to make Nick understand. "She runs for fun, Nick. She's young and healthy. Strong."

"And you aren't all those things?"

"I can barely walk at times, much less run. I don't want Kate—or anyone—having to deal with me on one of my bad days. Don't want her sitting home because I can't run or hike…or even friggin' dance with her."

He slugged back the rest of his drink and thumped the glass onto the table. "We came on a car accident after we went out to dinner one night, and I couldn't even drag one of the victims out of the car. I had to ask for help. What if that victim had been Kate?"

Nick's face tightened, his brows coming together. "You know, before I had my surgery, I felt the same way. Didn't want Tiggy saddled with me if things took a turn for the worse and I ended up in a wheelchair."

"But you didn't wind up in one."

"No, but I almost ruined my life by coming up with all kinds of depressing outcomes—none of which were based on reality."

"That's where you and I are different, Nick. Because my depressing outcome is very real. This leg is never going to get any better."

"And yet you're a doctor. A damn good one, from what I've seen. Your patients don't need you to jump hurdles or play hopscotch. And neither does Kate. At least, not the Kate that I got to know over the last couple of weeks. She cares about you, too. I could see it. Saw the way you smiled each other. Tiggy noticed it, as well."

Great, it seemed like the whole world knew his secret, including Laisse and some of the others at the hospital. Maybe it was time to own up to it. At least to himself.

He loved the woman. He had no idea when it had happened or why. But he did. It's why he'd had to let her go.

"She's gone. So there's your answer."

"I think she left *because* she cared. I didn't even realize it until you two were at the house and she got this funny look on her face when I mentioned our little agreement." His hand wrapped around his glass in a fist. "I've kicked myself so many times for saying that in front of her. But it just came out, and once it was said, there was no way to take it back."

"You didn't mess anything up. I just couldn't see any future for us."

"Because you're a damn fool. Just like I almost was." Nick leaned forward. "If you don't try to make this right, I think you'll regret it."

Maybe.

His friend sighed. "Don't make me regret fighting to save your leg that day. There were other men who weren't so lucky. You think they don't deserve a shot at happiness? You think the married ones should leave their wives and go off and live in a cave somewhere?"

Anger flared in his chest. "Of course not, but this is not the same."

"You're right. It's not." Nick slid his glass to the side and got as close to being in Luke's face as he could with a table between them. "You're a whole lot better off than some of the men I worked on. So maybe it's time you stopped feeling so damned sorry for yourself and started living your life…before it's too late. Before you lose a whole lot more than a chunk of your leg."

Luke's anger morphed into fury. "Back off, Nick. This is none of your business."

"Like hell it's not. Kate is my daughter." He leaned

back with a sigh and dug out his wallet, tossing a couple of bills onto the table. "I can't tell you what to do. But I'm asking you to think about it. Don't throw away something good—someone you care about—just because you're afraid of what the future might hold. You never know, Luke. It might just hold something pretty damn terrific."

CHAPTER TWENTY

IN THROUGH THE NOSE, out through the mouth.

The incline on the hill was a killer, but Kate forced herself to power through —she was now past the three-mile mark. She pulled deep breaths in and blew them out in a rhythmic cycle that could hold the world at bay just a little while longer. A classic rock band pumped through her ear buds and kept her company, the lead singer whining about being done wrong by a lover.

Been there. Done that.

She'd constantly wanted to call Luke over the past two weeks. And tell him what? That she was coming back to England? That she'd take him any way she could get him?

No, she respected herself more than that. Nick had called a few days ago, saying he hoped she hadn't gotten the wrong idea about what he'd said on her last night in London.

Nope, she hadn't. In fact, he'd saved her from making a fool of herself. If Luke had wanted her, he'd have said something to try to make her stay. Instead, that car had been filled with silence. And it had spoken loudly enough to get his point across.

In through the nose. Out through the mouth.

Her normal jogging route was busy today, full of

businesspeople all hoping to burn off a few extra calories before the start of a new week. Kate's reasons for running had nothing to do with calories and everything to do with pain management.

She cleared the ridge of the hill and shortened her strides as she started down the other side.

Up ahead, along the left-hand side of the trail, she spied someone on one of the benches dotted along the running path. A cane was propped against the seat next to the man and his right leg was stretched out in front of him.

Strange.

Although the trail was paved with a fresh coat of asphalt, the five-mile track didn't usually attract anyone other than power walkers and joggers because it ran next to a canal and was flanked by woods on both sides. Her eyes clipped to the left as she passed the bench, and the air stuttered from her lungs. She ran a couple more steps before she faltered, her mind whirling. She stopped and swiped at a trickle of sweat on her temple, struggling to make sense of what she'd just seen.

That couldn't have been...

No. It couldn't.

She geared herself up to take off again, forcing herself not to look back, not to invite the crush of disappointment that would surely follow.

And then she heard her name.

Low. Familiar.

Unmistakable.

She turned round slowly, swallowing when she saw the man was on his feet, cane in hand.

Luke.

But how? Why?

She tried to say something but could think of nothing

that would explain his sudden appearance in Memphis. On *her* jogging trail.

And Luke didn't use a cane.

Or he hadn't. Had something happened?

She closed the space between them, still trying to catch her breath. "What's wrong? Your leg, is it—?"

"It's fine."

She plopped down on the bench, her muscles suddenly too shaky to support her weight. Luke eased down beside her, resting the cane between his legs.

Maybe she was suffering from oxygen deprivation or something. "You're supposed to be in London."

"I'm taking some time off."

Okay. That explained why he was in the States but not why he was *here.*

"Are you originally from Memphis?" She felt totally lost. Totally out of her element.

"Nope. Chicago." He flashed her a smile that made her insides warm.

He wasn't here to return her panties, because those had been given back ages ago. "You're going to have to help me out a little here, Luke. I'm not sure… Why are you in Memphis?"

"I came to find you."

He had? "But why?"

"To tell you Nick was wrong." His fingertips gripped the cane, turning it slightly before his eyes came up to meet hers. "I did agree to talk to you for him, but that had nothing to do with what went on between you and me."

"It—it didn't?" This was exactly what she'd wanted him to say that last night. And yet he hadn't. So why now?

"I should have said something as soon as we got

into the car, but it just seemed easier to let you think the worst of me."

"Because you didn't want to give me any reason to stay." The truth stole the air from her lungs, much like that proverbial wall that runners hit halfway through a marathon. And it hurt. Lord, how it hurt.

"No. I didn't want you to stay." He shifted in his seat until he actually faced her, his gaze trailing over her face. "It was stupid and cowardly. And I'm not proud of letting you leave like that. I want to try to set things straight."

He'd come an awful long way just to do that.

"Okay. But I—"

"I'm not quite finished." His chest rose as he took a deep breath. "I also want to ask you to give me another chance. To come back to London with me."

Her mouth popped open and she stared at him. She slicked some loose strands of hair back from her face, suddenly very aware that her green T-shirt was sweat-soaked and she was a mess. "What?"

"Nick seems to think you might care about me. And I know I care about you." He dragged a hand through his hair. "Hell, that's not what I want to say. I *love* you, dammit. I want you with me."

Despite the shock rolling through her system, his rough words made her smile. They were about as far from the cool, seductive lover she'd known in London as they could get. As was the cane.

She sidestepped his shocking statement, needing time to think. "Why are you using a cane, if your leg is okay?"

"Because I've finally accepted that I need it. I don't use it at work, but it takes some of the strain off at home." He smiled. "And it's a big help when walking up crazy hills along a jogging path."

That's right. She was at the three-mile mark, which meant Luke had walked almost two miles to get where he was.

As if reading her mind, he nodded. "I was going to keep walking until I found you but realized my leg wasn't going to make it any further." His smile faded. "That's another thing. Even if you agree to give me another chance, you need to know my leg will never be any better than it is right now."

"I'm not sure why that's even…" Her heart flipped in her chest, her eyes filling with tears. "You think I care about your leg?"

"I can't run with you, Kate. And I want to. More than anything." His voice turned gravelly in a way that tore at her insides.

"I never wanted you for a running partner. Never." She cupped his face and leaned in so he could see the truth in her eyes. "I love you. I do. Everything about you. Including your leg."

Luke dragged her to him, his mouth covering hers in an instant. His long fiery kiss had none of his usual smoothness. It was rough and raw—just like his words had been—and she couldn't get enough. Because *this* was Luke. The real Luke, full of insecurities and despair…and capable of happiness, just like any other human being. He was just a man.

She vaguely heard his cane clattering to the ground, but she wrapped her arms around his neck and held him to her, afraid that if she let him go, she'd find he wasn't here at all. The breath she'd just finished catching was off and running all over again, but this time she didn't care. All she wanted was this man…this crazy mixed-up—

"Get a room!" The half-amused yell came from the trail next to them, and she pulled her head back slightly, while keeping her arms around Luke's neck. A young man had just run by them, his long strides carrying him on down the trail and out of sight as he turned a corner.

"I think he wants us to get a room," she whispered, as she turned back toward Luke

He grinned. "And what about you, Kate? Is that what you want?" She heard the question loud and clear, and her heart sang in her chest.

She leaned forward and kissed him again. "I don't want just a room. I want the whole house."

His breath left his lips on a sigh. "You've got it. Anything you want."

"In that case, I'll call my dad and let him know I'll be out for a while."

"Your dad already knows, I think. I called him and explained the situation. He told me where I could find you."

"In that case, I know a little place we can be alone."

Luke picked up his cane and climbed to his feet. "We'd better get started, then. It'll take me a while to get back down the path."

"There's no hurry." She took his free hand in hers. "We've got all the time in the world."

EPILOGUE

"SHE'S BEAUTIFUL." KATE'S voice held a note of awe as she gazed down at the newborn in her arms, daring to stroke a tiny hand.

Luke perched on the arm of the chair his fiancée currently occupied. "Yes, she is." He dropped a kiss on her head. "You're going to have to give her back, though."

"I know. I can hardly believe I have a little sister."

That was easy for Luke to believe. What was harder was that the smart, beautiful woman next to him had actually agreed to marry him—on his first proposal, even though he'd been prepared to ask her over and over again, if necessary. As long as it took to convince her that he loved her.

He'd offered to practice medicine back in the States but Kate had wanted to come back with him so he could finish out his year at the hospital in London. And as a side benefit he got to see her any time he wanted to as she was working in the physical therapy center.

They'd both been asked to stay on at the hospital when his term ended, and Luke wasn't sure what they were going to do. He would leave that up to Kate. She had her father's Parkinson's to think of. The new regimen of medicine had slowed the progress of the disease but until a cure could be found, it was always there—waiting in the wings.

Luke didn't care where they ended up, as long as they were together.

He eyed the cane propped on the chair next to him with a rueful smile. Who would have guessed that, instead of making his leg weaker, it had made it more tolerant of work? He got through his day without it for the most part, but it allowed his remaining muscles to recuperate between shifts. Kate—putting on her PT hat—had said it was similar to a runner sitting out a day or two in order to let the stressed muscle fibers regenerate. The strategies that worked for her worked for him, as well.

Although he didn't run with her, he did go to the park and sit on a bench, enjoying the sight of her lithe frame as she powered past him and blew him a kiss. And sometimes there was a special reward for him when they got back home to his apartment—when she'd let him slowly peel off her sweaty workout gear and join her in the shower.

Something he'd better not think about right now. Especially not with a baby in the room.

The door to the restroom opened and Nick and Tiggy came out, the new mother wheeling her IV stand along with her. She looked good, a lot better than twelve hours ago, when the obstetrician—a worried frown between his brows—had ordered an emergency C-section, saying the baby's heart rate was slowing down too much. It had been a good call because the cord had been wrapped around the infant's neck, each contraction tightening it and reducing the baby's blood flow.

Tiggy glanced over at them, bent slightly at the waist

to keep pressure off her sutures. "Ugh. That was not fun. Thanks for holding her for me."

"I told you we needed to wait for a nurse," Nick chided softly.

"I *am* a nurse. Besides, there are two doctors right here in the room."

Nick helped her settle back in her bed with an amused sigh. "The longer they keep you, the better."

"Oh, no. I'm ready to leave. I have a wedding to plan."

Kate stood and carried the baby over to her, gently placing the child in her arms. "The wedding is still four months away. You'll be exhausted for the next couple of months so you need to take it easy."

"She's going to be a good baby, aren't you, love?" She gazed down at the baby with adoration. They'd named her Poppy, in honor of fallen soldiers everywhere.

"Well, we'd better let you get some rest." Kate stood and held her hand out for Luke, who ignored it, wrapping his left arm around her waist instead and tugging her close.

Nick grinned. "Thank you for coming. It means a lot to both of us."

"I wouldn't have missed it. Besides, this is where I belong." She wrapped her arms around Luke's waist and returned his squeeze with a smile.

Picking up his cane, he put it to the floor and took a step toward the door. Kate matched his pace perfectly, trying neither to push him forward nor slow him down. His hand relished the warm, solid feel of the wood beneath his hand. Kate had bought him a fancy carved cane in the States with a secret engraving beneath the handle that no one knew about but them: *Luke ♥s Kate*.

Truer words had never been written.

Who would have thought what he'd deemed a sign of weakness had actually become a symbol of strength? Because it was only after he'd accepted his limitations that he'd been able to open himself up to true and lasting happiness. And been free to embrace it.

With a woman who was strong and courageous enough for both of them.

* * * * *

Mills & Boon® Hardback

September 2013

ROMANCE

MEDICAL

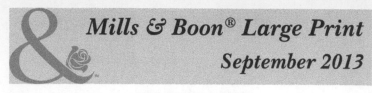

Mills & Boon® Large Print
September 2013

ROMANCE

A Rich Man's Whim	Lynne Graham
A Price Worth Paying?	Trish Morey
A Touch of Notoriety	Carole Mortimer
The Secret Casella Baby	Cathy Williams
Maid for Montero	Kim Lawrence
Captive in his Castle	Chantelle Shaw
Heir to a Dark Inheritance	Maisey Yates
Anything but Vanilla...	Liz Fielding
A Father for Her Triplets	Susan Meier
Second Chance with the Rebel	Cara Colter
First Comes Baby...	Michelle Douglas

HISTORICAL

The Greatest of Sins	Christine Merrill
Tarnished Amongst the Ton	Louise Allen
The Beauty Within	Marguerite Kaye
The Devil Claims a Wife	Helen Dickson
The Scarred Earl	Elizabeth Beacon

MEDICAL

NYC Angels: Redeeming The Playboy	Carol Marinelli
NYC Angels: Heiress's Baby Scandal	Janice Lynn
St Piran's: The Wedding!	Alison Roberts
Sydney Harbour Hospital: Evie's Bombshell	Amy Andrews
The Prince Who Charmed Her	Fiona McArthur
His Hidden American Beauty	Connie Cox

ROMANCE

MEDICAL

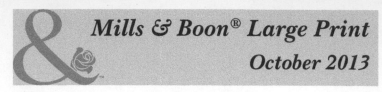

Mills & Boon® Large Print
October 2013

ROMANCE

The Sheikh's Prize	Lynne Graham
Forgiven but not Forgotten?	Abby Green
His Final Bargain	Melanie Milburne
A Throne for the Taking	Kate Walker
Diamond in the Desert	Susan Stephens
A Greek Escape	Elizabeth Power
Princess in the Iron Mask	Victoria Parker
The Man Behind the Pinstripes	Melissa McClone
Falling for the Rebel Falcon	Lucy Gordon
Too Close for Comfort	Heidi Rice
The First Crush Is the Deepest	Nina Harrington

HISTORICAL

Reforming the Viscount	Annie Burrows
A Reputation for Notoriety	Diane Gaston
The Substitute Countess	Lyn Stone
The Sword Dancer	Jeannie Lin
His Lady of Castlemora	Joanna Fulford

MEDICAL

NYC Angels: Unmasking Dr Serious	Laura Iding
NYC Angels: The Wallflower's Secret	Susan Carlisle
Cinderella of Harley Street	Anne Fraser
You, Me and a Family	Sue MacKay
Their Most Forbidden Fling	Melanie Milburne
The Last Doctor She Should Ever Date	Louisa George